DEEP SPACE
CELEBRATION

James Van Hise

A PIONEER BOOK

Recently Released Pioneer Books. . .

MTV: MUSIC YOU CAN SEE	ISBN#1-55698-355-7
TREK: THE NEXT GENERATION CREW BOOK	ISBN#1-55698-363-8
TREK: THE PRINTED ADVENTURES	ISBN#1-55698-365-5
THE CLASSIC TREK CREW BOOK	ISBN#1-55698-368-9
TREK VS THE NEXT GENERATION	ISBN#1-55698-370-0
TREK: THE NEXT GENERATION TRIBUTE BOOK	ISBN#1-55698-366-2
THE HOLLYWOOD CELEBRITY DEATH BOOK	ISBN#1-55698-369-7
LET'S TALK: AMERICA'S FAVORITE TV TALK SHOW HOSTS	ISBN#1-55698-364-6
HOT-BLOODED DINOSAUR MOVIES	ISBN#1-55698~365-4
BONANZA: THE UNOFFICIAL STORY OF THE PONDEROSA	ISBN#1-55698-359-X

Exciting new titles soon to be released

THE KUNG FU BOOK	ISBN#1-55698-328-X
TREK: THE DEEP SPACE CELEBRATION	ISBN#1-55698 330-1
TREK: THE DEEP SPACE CREW BOOK	ISBN#1-55698-335-2
MARRIAGE & DIVORCE -HOLLYWOOD STYLE	ISBN#1-55698-333-6
TREK: THE ENCYCLOPEDIA	ISBN#1-55698-331-X
THE LITTLE HOUSE COMPANION	ISBN#1-55698-332-8

PUBLISHER: Hal Schuster   **DESIGNER:** Ben Long   **EDITOR:** David Lessnick

Library of Congress Cataloging-in-Publication Data
James Van Hise, 1959—

Deep Space: A Celebration

1. Deep Space: A Celebration (television, popular culture)
I. Title

Published by Pioneer Books, Inc., 5715 N. Balsam Rd., Las Vegas, NV, 89130.

First Printing, 1994

Table of Contents

AT THE EDGE OF THE FINAL FRONTIER

DEEP SPACE NINE is a serieS poised and waiting for real wonders to unfold. Out there, so close and yet so far, lies the Gamma Quadrant just beyond the wormhole. But on this side of the wormhole, in the Alpha Quadrant, is the space station at the gateway to the wormhole. People come and go on the space station, but attention is inevitably drawn to the wormhole itself and what it represents.

The wormhole is where everyone is really going to and coming from. Trips taken into it, in "Battle Lines" and "The Alternate," have offered tantalizing glimpses of what is there. And the episodes "Rules Of Acquisition" and "Sanctuary" have established the off-stage presence of a race or a group called the Dominion who are powerful and yet whose ethical standing in the order of things has yet to be delineated. But they are out there, in the Gamma Quadrant, and increasingly that is where the show keeps pointing while merely observing how everyone else reacts to the dynamic new possibilities it presents.

One of the secrets in the Gamma Quadrant is the origin of Odo and his

race of shape-shifters. Surely some of the aliens coming through the wormhole would be familiar with the species he represents, but none yet have truly revealed anything truthful. Odo was apparently launched through the wormhole from the Gamma Quadrant, perhaps to save him from something. Is Odo the last of his kind? Even he must wonder. What is keeping him on Deep Space Nine and preventing him from going off on his own to track down his roots? We don't know. It is an obvious question which hasn't been an-swered or even explored.

This book attempts to answer and explore a lot of questions as we cover the portrayal of women, religion and relation-ships on DEEP SPACE NINE as well as provid-ing an exhaustive glos-sary of the terms and names used in the first season of the series. They've invented a lot

just for this series, as you'll see. Our episode guide also picks up where our previous vol-ume left off but we don't just cover the plots but examine them as well, reviewing what we find there.

So step aboard the runabout as we take off for the Alpha Quadrant and the space station known as Deep Space Nine!

—-James Van Hise

In the original '60s Star Trek, the only regular female characters were Uhura, the Communications Officer, and Nurse Chapel. Much more has been achieved over the years with the female characters, although it has remained an uphill struggle.

THE WOMEN OF DEEP SPACE NINE
by Wendy Rathbone

Women in *Star Trek* have come a long way since the days of Kirk, Spock and the Constitution class Enterprise. In that early Federation, women were not allowed to command starships (according to the Classic Trek episode "Turnabout Intruder") and were considered independent, powerful and free because they were beautiful, sexy and promiscuous. Kirk's womanizer reputation had a lot of help when so-called intelligent women would throw themselves at him every third week.

If a woman was sly, tough, isolated, independent from men, then something was wrong with her society, her life, and her mind. Note Kara in "Spock's Brain," Lenore in "The Conscience of the King," most especially Janice in "Turnabout Intruder," Miranda in "Is There In Truth No Beauty?", Nancy Hedford in "Metamorphosis," Dr. Dehner in "Where No Man Has Gone Before," and numerous episodes where women are the ones who play secretary, hand Kirk fuel consumption reports, bring trays of beverages to the men on the bridge, etc.

Even the seeming exception of

Number One in "The Menagerie" shows her as a cold, un-emotional character, as if she couldn't have risen to her position if she had allowed her feminine side to show. Kirk had to go all the way back in time to find a woman who was both feminine and intelligent, his equal per se, in the form of Edith Keeler from "The City On The Edge Of Forever." But forward in the 23rd century, we won't even begin to discuss the sexist uniforms which showed a lot of leg.

The Long, Slow Growth of Deanna Troi

This attitude improved somewhat in *The Next Generation*. Deanna Troi, whom I disliked immensely at first, has grown on me. Not only has she managed to keep her femininity while holding a very powerful position on board the Enterprise, but she appears to be admired by the men for her intellect first, and her beauty second. This is quite refreshing. While Kirk might have gawked out of the corner of his eye at her, Picard has never been seen to do so. So not only is there an improvement on the women in this series, but the men's attitudes have evolved as well.

Deanna is a person, and her beauty does not automatically mean she is a sex symbol. Nor was that the case with Tasha Yar. And Dr. Beverly Crusher has grown to become a whole person as well. Unfortunately, Marina Sirtis, who plays Deanna Troi, has stated her frustration over the inability for *Star Trek* writers to create strong female characters. So there is still a way to go. She sees that her role, though respected, is limited and can't help but see that it is because she is small, pretty, soft-spoken, and non-aggressive.

Luckily, what has been

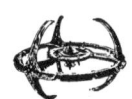

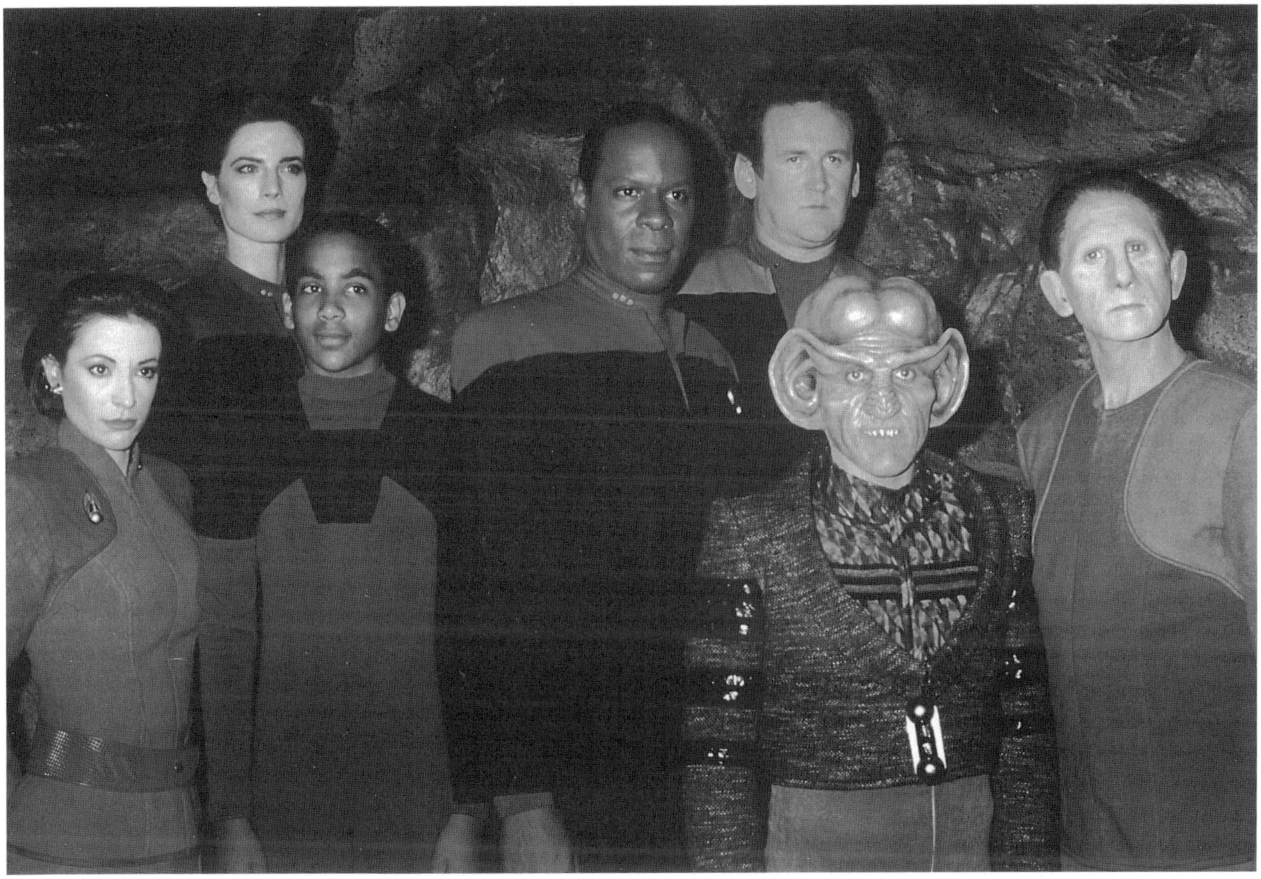

Photo © 1994 Alvert L. Ortega

Cast of Star Trek: Deep Space Nine *at a Paramount Studios' Press Conference.*

learned from *Next Generation* through mistakes and blunders has helped to improve the plight of women in *Deep Space Nine*. I still have a few quibbles, which will be addressed, but for the most part, this series treats men and women equally, as it does all races. I'm not saying that the people of *Deep Space Nine* are free of individual prejudices. They are not. But this makes the series 'human,' and the characters are more credible. It is a conceivable improvement over *Next Generation's* rather bland, boring approach that everyone automatically gets along with and accepts everyone else among the primary crew members. That's simply unrealistic. So the fact that the characters of *Deep Space Nine* are not all the same in

Nana Visitor at Universal for the cast Q&A with fans.

Photo c 1994 Alvert L. Ortega

the way they view others and their outside 'world' makes for some very interesting confrontations.

The Former Terrorist

Major Kira Nerys, a Bajoran woman, was also part of the resistance freedom fighters against the Cardassians when they occupied Bajor. She is Commander Benjamin Sisko's first officer and is as strong and capable as any of the characters on the show, but she has her faults, too. She's quick to judge, tends to see issues as black and white, and is often motivated by anger, but also by the need to see justice done. This not only makes her an interesting person, but a character that has great potential to grow and to evolve with the spirit of the series.

Her aggressiveness, however, is attributed to her Bajoran heritage.

Bajoran women are aggressive, Nana Visitor told Starlog in 1993. "That's where the difficulty in playing her comes in. I'm constantly on guard against having Kira come across as a man. Her strength is a woman's strength, and I'm working very hard on making that strength come across that way."

That statement is a little disturbing to me in that I'm not quite sure what the ultimate difference is between male and female aggression. If she means that Kira is not going to punch someone out as the traditional male stereotype might, I have not seen evidence of this. Kira can hold her own in a fight, and in fact has been seen to take down a few men in her time with hand to hand combat skills. I don't think that makes her look particularly masculine, and it is admirable.

If she means that her aggression will come across in the stereotypical feminine way which includes the more indirect way of dealing with things such as gossiping to turn people against each other, manipulation, using the cold shoulder, well . . . that too has been seen in her understandable irritation with the Ferengi bar owner Quark. But to be fair, she has no problem in confronting Quark when it suits her purposes. All in all, I believe her character is a strong one, and any labeling put onto her such as 'masculine' or 'butch' would seem to be the result of ignorance about the range both men and women occupy in life.

The Hollywood Syndrome

The problem with strong female characters is not limited to *Star Trek*. It is a Hollywood problem. In another Starlog article, Nana Visitor states, "I was attracted to the script right away by the strength of my character. Actually, both Kira and Dax are powerful women. To play a strong woman on television, or in any medium, really, is unusual, very rare, and it's a huge joy for me." The fact that *Star Trek* in all its incarnations has come far in its treatment of women cannot be ignored. It's been a fight. We can't blame Gene Roddenberry's alleged sexism from the first series for all of it when the treatment of women in Classic Trek quite probably involved much more than Gene's own views. Hollywood has always had an unrealistic view of the 'real' woman, and breaking out of the Barbie mold should always be applauded. *Star Trek* has done a lot to break the mold.

However, things are not perfect on the *Deep Space Nine* set. I found it a little frustrating, when doing research for this piece, to come across the information that Terry Farrell, who plays the Trill Jadzia Dax, had her makeup changed by higher 'male' powers because the original Trill makeup appliance covered her beautiful face too much. Though it is flattering to be called beautiful, and no one is arguing Farrell is a handsome woman, the reasons for changing the Trill makeup appear on the surface to be sexist ones. You don't see them changing Klingon or other alien makeup on men just because the man underneath is handsome and should be seen.

But to be fair, the symbiotic worm inside Jadzia was also changed from the original *Next Generation* episode's depiction in "The Host." The symbiote is smaller, redesigned by Michael Westmore. But why the redesign? I haven't a clue.

Terry Farrell at Golden Apple Comics to promote Clive Barker's
Hellraiser III: Hell on Earth.   **Photo c 1994 Alvert L. Ortega**

The Old, Young Trill

Jadzia Dax is an interesting character in that she is a Trill, which means the sexless symbiote inside her has experienced both male and female lives and retains those memories. She is, conceivably, a character who could comprise the best of

Nana Visitor attending the Cast Q&A session at Universal Studios.

Photo © 1994 Alvert L. Ortega

both worlds. When she was in her male form, Curzon, she was best friends with Sisko and was also his mentor. Their relationship has not really changed, much to Sisko's credit, for handling her new form with the respect due her, but he has been honest in pointing out to her that her new form is rather distracting since she is both attractive and female, and that he's not used to relating to that form. This is not sexism on the part of Sisko, but an honest reaction considering that Jadzia, the host, does have her own personality and that the symbiote, Dax, is a different person in the sense that Jadzia and her personality is now a big part of him/it/her.

I have wondered, though; is Dax automatically treated as an equal because she was once a man, and because she is very old, as well as not human? (For that matter, Kira isn't human either.)

Is it easier for men to write strong roles for non-human, alien females than for human ones? This is just a question I put to the reader, not to accuse any writers or producers of any applicable 'ism or 'ist attitude.

One thing that has really impressed me about Dax is that through her life experience she appears to have completely rid herself of any intolerance toward others. Because she is female and beautiful, she must put up with the brunt of Quark's often sexist jokes, but she doesn't care one bit. In fact, she likes Quark—even understands him. She enjoys playing cards and other games with the Ferengi, and has even admitted she finds the Ferengi race one of the more entertaining species she has ever encountered.

Because she doesn't react to their culturally sexist attitudes, the Ferengi, in particular, Quark, have come to accept and respect her. She has no problem getting along with them because she does not allow herself to be offended. Kira, on the other hand, is so quick to take offense that she just asks for more teasing. She does not understand or accept Ferengi culture, and though their snide attitudes are not limited to women and include each other (note how terribly Quark treats his brother, Rom), she can't just ignore them and let them be.

The Long Suffering Keiko

Another female character on *Deep Space Nine* is Keiko, played by Rosalind Chao. While the roles of Kira and Dax have been a definite improvement over other Trek female roles, Keiko is a step backwards. This could have to do with the fact that her character has never really been fully developed from her first appearance in *Next Generation* through *Deep Space Nine*. Keiko was a biologist on the Enterprise who gave up her career there to move with her husband, Miles O'Brien, to *Deep Space Nine*. They have a young daughter, Molly, and it appears that Keiko is the primary caregiver there.

This in itself is not at all sexist. I have no problem with women devoting quality time as parents to their children. It also makes sense that if O'Brien had the better job, or the better job offer, then they as a family unit would decide to move to accommodate that. But what I can't understand is why Keiko couldn't find anything to do on *Deep Space Nine* that would utilize her science education. Not only is the station located right near the wormhole leading to a quadrant of the

Rosalyn Chao at the "Joy Luck" premiere.
Photo c 1994 Alvert L. Ortega

galaxy yet unexplored, filled with planets to discover, but it is also stationed near Bajor, which is having a great problem with famines. I would think Bajor would need all the scientific help they could get to solve this problem. Keiko would be eminently qualified, and just because she's human I don't think working with Bajorans would be a problem.

On the other hand, perhaps Keiko wanted to give up her job. Perhaps she hated biology. If that is the case, the writers could have a script dealing with that, and addressing her mid-life change in career. That is interesting. It would make her character more three-dimensional. Instead, they have Keiko, admittedly concerned for her daughter's welfare on a backwater sort of 'little house on the prairie' colony station, decide to open a school and teach the diverse group of *Deep*

Space Nine children. This makes sense and is a generous move on her part, and a good decision if she wants to both work and remain close to her daughter.

Was Keiko Demoted?

But there is a problem. Molly is preschool age; too young to attend the classes Keiko teaches. Perhaps Keiko takes her to school with her, but this has not yet been shown. And now, suddenly, recent episodes had Keiko conveniently away from the station on an extended visit with her parents on Earth. So what happened to the school? In the episode "In The Hands Of The Prophets," it gets blown up, but that doesn't mean school stops, does it? Is there a separation for Miles and Keiko in the future? Is their marriage on the rocks? I personally think the reasons for removing Keiko from *Deep Space Nine* is be-

cause the writers don't like her (she's a human woman!), don't know how to handle her, find her boring, etc. (Viewers probably do, too.)

The last time Keiko was seen before leaving for Earth was when she and Miles temporarily take in a Cardassian orphan. Keiko is seen serving up dinner to the family. Poor Keiko. She was once a starship officer and while I'm not saying taking care of a family is anything to be ashamed of, well, you don't see the men in *Star Trek* making these kinds of choices! Sisko is able to be both a father and a commander. Worf can have a son and be a high-ranking Enterprise bridge officer. When Keiko did finally reappear, in "Rivals," all her scenes are of preparing dinner and trying to soothe her husband's wounded ego when he gets trounced playing racquetball. She doesn't interact with any other

character in the storyline.

If Keiko does leave *Deep Space Nine*, I hope she leaves the little girl with O'Brien. I like to see the men having responsibility for their children. I like that Sisko and Worf have sons. Leaving O'Brien in the singular care of his daughter would only add to the breaking of sexist stereotypes here.

I like the depiction of Bajorans on *Deep Space Nine*. The men and women appear to be pretty equal in anything they might want to do. Both sexes hold high-ranking positions in government and religious organizations. There is no differentiation seen between male and female capabilities in being soldiers, officers, priests, terrorists, business persons, farmers and renegades.

Terry Farrell (Dax) at Universal Studios.
Photo c 1994 Chris Flicker

The Quirks of Ferengi Family Life

The Ferengi, on the other hand, keep their women naked and submissive. This actually led to a great *Deep Space Nine* episode about Ferengi sexism where a Ferengi female disguises herself as a male and succeeds in business as well as, if not better, than the males. When she proves she is as intelligent and capable as any man, and then reveals the truth about herself to Quark (whom she falls in love with in, unfortunately, stereotypical female fashion) and to the Grand Nagus, this does not change anything. The Nagus is horrified and denies her successes (even though they were profitable for him) as ever having occurred.

Ferengi females appear to have a long way to go for equality. But she did leave Quark with a rather puzzled, contemplative look on his face. He actually cared for her, even before he knew she was a female, and it does appear that he might have learned a small lesson in seeing the person first, the biological plumbing second. Whe-ther he puts that lesson to work in his life is another matter. I doubt he'll ever stop teasing Kira. But then that might come to be a more personal war instead of a sexist one.

All in all, *Deep Space Nine* offers women equal opportunity, and the writers of the show have shown great efforts in trying to handle the 'war of the sexes' with fairness and sensitivity. With only a few remaining problems, *Deep Space Nine* has warped light years ahead of Classic Trek in showing fair and positive female role models. In fact, *Star Trek* as it is seen now, with women as starship captains, has even surpassed most of the Hollywood mentality that still depicts frozen

stereotypes a little too often. My hat is off to the writers and producers. And from its earliest inception until now, *Star Trek* has been a great influence in my life. I'll always love it, whether the women wear miniskirts or short hair, become underground terrorists or family caregivers, whether they are human, Betazoid, Bajoran or symbiote. It's all great fun.

Terry Farrell at Cast Q&A at Universal Studios.

Photo c 1994 Alvert L. Ortega

The universe explored in all forms of Star Trek *is much more than space battles and encounters with alien races. There is a human, personal side which has always figured into the tales it told.*

FAMILIES AND RELATIONSHIPS IN TREK
by Kay Doty

Family members and enduring relationships were largely ignored in the original Star Trek series, but this has gradually changed in both *The Next Generation* and *Deep Space Nine*. While it would lead to confusion (not to mention possible cancellation) to have family reunions interrupting the daily schedule, it is assumed that the characters do have private lives. Giving the viewers a glimpse of these off duty lives adds a flavor and a sense of reality to the show.

In some of the early episodes of the original series several scenes indicated that Captain Kirk had a romantic interest in Yeoman Rand (Grace Lee Whitney). At the insistence of the network, Whitney was dropped from the cast after the series thirteenth episode, "The Conscience of the King." This allowed a handsome, unfettered captain the freedom to become the galactic lothario.

From that point on there were no continuing relationships during the first five-year mission. Kirk did have a number of romances but none survived more than one episode. The most memorable was Edith Keeler (Joan

Collins) in "The City On The Edge of Forever," who died at story's end. On Deep Space Nine, Commander Sisko's wife Jennifer died even before the series began, but she was given a graceful flashback so that we had something to remember her by.

Kirk's Past Catches Up With Him

Dr. Carol Marcus, (Bibi Besch) apparently the love of Kirk's life before he became captain of the Enterprise, did not appear on screen until *Star Trek* II: *The Wrath of Khan*, although she had been mentioned in a novel.

Accompanying Carol Marcus into the world of Star Trek was her son, David (Merritt Butrick) who was initially unaware that Kirk was his father. After some early hostility when David first learned of his relationship with Kirk, the two became close. Unfortu-

nately David was killed by Klingons midway through The Search For Spock, and in her grief, Carol refused to see or talk with Kirk again.

Carol Marcus has not appeared in subsequent films; however in the novelization of *Star Trek* VI: *The Undiscovered Country*, she and Kirk were reconciled.

We are told little about Kirk's family. He mentioned a brother, George, whom he calls Sam in "What Are Little Girls Made Of?" In the last episode of the first season, "Operation: Annihilate," George and his wife Aurelan (Joan Swift) are killed by flying amoeba-like aliens. Their son, Peter, was the sole family survivor.

Vulcan Entanglements

Much more was revealed about Spock's family when, in the second season's "Journey To Babel," his parents (Jane Wyatt as

Amanda and Mark Lenard as Sarek) come aboard the Enterprise. The couple, particularly Sarek, became so popular that they remained a part of the Star Trek universe. Although Amanda's only other appearance was in *Star Trek IV: The Voyage Home*, Sarek was in *Star Trek* III, IV, VI and two *Next Generation* episodes—"Sarek" and "Unification: Part I."

And of course in *Star Trek V: The Final Frontier* we learn that Spock has a renegade brother named Sybok.

Then there was T'Pring. According to Vulcan custom, children's future marriages were arranged for them, at the age of seven, by their parents. As an adult, T'Pring was no longer enamored with Spock, and arranged for a challenge match that not only released her from the commitment, but nearly cost Kirk his life.

Spock's only romantic entanglements were the result of events beyond his control, such as the spores in "This Side Of Paradise." Another encounter occurred when he and McCoy beamed down to the planet Sarpeidon ("All Our Yesterdays") and found themselves hurled 5,000 years into the past.

Spock reverted to the emotional ways of his ancestors, falling in love with the beautiful and lonely Zarabeth (Mariette Hartley). Unfortunately their love was doomed, for Zarabeth could not leave her world, and Spock would have died had he remained with her.

In "The Enterprise Incident," while Kirk was stealing the cloaking device, Spock entertained, and was entertained by, the Romulan Commander (Joanne Linville). As the story unfolded it became apparent Spock's interest went beyond duty. One is left to wonder what might have happened, had Spock had a bit longer to dally with the beautiful commander.

McCoy and Company

Dr. McCoy was pretty closed-mouthed about his family. Some place in his background was a divorced wife and a daughter named Joanna, but they never appeared on screen, although there was an unproduced third season script which featured McCoy's daughter.

The good doctor did find romance on at least one occasion. In "For The World Is Hollow And I Have Touched The Sky," he actually got married. Believing he had a terminal illness, McCoy joined a landing party beaming to the asteroid Yonada. There he was captivated by the High Priestess Natira. She returned his love and asked him to marry her. He did so after explaining that he had but a year to live. After the ceremony he learned

the cure to his disease could be found on Yonada.

Relieved that his life wasn't about to end, he returned to the ship with the remedy—leaving his marriage vows behind.

Even less is known about the other characters. Lt. Uhura was never romantically involved with anyone, nor was any mention of her family made. The same holds true for Lieutenant Sulu and Ensign Chekov, although we did learn that the latter was an only child. Not much more information about Scotty was ever revealed. His nephew, Peter Preston (Ike Eisenmann) was one of the cadets training on the Enterprise under the command of Captain Spock (The Wrath of Khan) He was one of many who died during the battle with Khan.

Colm Meany with daughter Brenda at Universal.

Photo c 1994 Alvert L. Ortega

Montgomery Scott

Scotty didn't do much better in the romance department. Although his first love was always his beloved engines, he did become infatuated with Lieutenant Carolyn Palamas, who dumped him for the god Apollo in "Who Mourns For Adonais."

Later in "The Lights Of Zetar" the engineer becomes enraptured with Lieutenant Mira Romaine, and the feeling is mutual. She had been

Ciroc Lofton with Avery Brooks at the Universal Cast Q&A.
Photo c 1994 Alvert L. Ortega

sent to the Enterprise to oversee the transfer of new equipment to Memory Alpha. During a storm the "lights" entered Mira's body and refused to leave. Scotty was instrumental in saving her life, and asked her to remain on the Enterprise with him. Mira was tempted, but her orders called for her to return to Memory Alpha to repair damage caused by the storm.

In fairness to Gene Roddenberry and the powers behind the series, there was no reason to believe that a program that barely survived three seasons would take on a new life in syndication. Nor could they have known that millions of fans would want all the intimate details of their hero's lives.

To supply these details nearly a hundred professional novels have been written, and countless amateur novels and stories by fans.

Families in Space

Fans soon learned that Roddenberry didn't make the same mistake regarding the personal lives of his characters with *Star Trek:The Next Generation*. He set the stage for families by having family and civilian quarters "built" into the newest Enterprise, 1701-D. This left the door open for stories involving families of the crew.

In the initial episode, "Encounter At Farpoint," the widowed Dr. Beverly Crusher arrived on board with her teenage son, Wesley. In addition, her husband, Jack had been Captain Picard's best friend. Beverly and Picard remained close friends, and only their positions aboard ship prevented the friendship from turning into a romance.

Both had other romances as the series progressed, but only Picard's encounter with the irrepressible Vash (Jennifer Hetrick) did not end with one episode. She first appeared in "Captain's Holiday," and later in "QPid." Although he hasn't seen her since, when she left him to flit off with Q, Vash's nature is such that she could reappear at any time, and did on *Deep Space Nine* (although not in the company of Picard).

Details were revealed about Picard's early life when he returned to his home in France to recuperate from his encounter with the Borg, "Family." During this reunion with his brother Robert (Jeremy Kemp), sister-in-law, Marie (Samantha Eggar), and nephew Rene (David Tristin Birkin), many events in the brothers' competitive childhood's were revealed.

Riker and Troi

Commander William Riker was also surprised during "Encounter At Farpoint," when he arrived on the Enterprise to take up his duties as first officer. It came as a distinct shock to discover that his old love, Counselor Deanna Troi, was aboard. They maintain the illusion that they had become just 'good friends,' but throughout the series a mystique surrounded the pair that leaves fans wondering if maybe there might be just a bit more than friendship.

Like Picard and Crusher, Riker and Troi have had one episode love affairs, but their only enduring bond seems to be with each other.

Troi's exasperating, widowed mother Lwaxana (Majel Barrett) was introduced in the first season episode "Haven," and continued in a reoccurring role. Although initially portrayed as a cartoonish, comedy relief character, in the last three years storylines have shown other sides to her as well which have deepened her humanity to richer levels.

Riker had to wait until the second season episode "The Icarus Factor" to encounter his father, Kyle, from whom he had been estranged for fifteen years. The meeting between the two was more on the order of a confrontation, but by the end of the episode they had resolved their differences. Will's mother died when he was a child.

In the seventh season, "Second Chances," Riker had the unique, and unnerving experience of learning that due to a transporter malfunction, a duplicate of himself had materialized. The "twin" remained passionately in love with Deanna. She reluctantly declined his marriage proposal, for the time. But "Thomas" Riker lives on, although posted to a different Starfleet vessel. So like it or not, Will Riker now has a twin brother.

Avery Brooks at the '93 Hollywood Christmas Parade.
Photo c 1994 Alvert L. Ortega

Ciroc Lofton at the Hollywood Christmas Parade.
Photo c 1994 Alvert L. Ortega

Worf's Extended Family

Worf was disconcerted when a former love in the person of Ambassador K'Ehleyr (Susie Plakson) came aboard the Enterprise in "The Emissary." The couple resolved their differences, but K'Ehleyr refused his marriage proposal, but according to Klingon custom, they parted as mates.

They did not see each other again until approximately five years later when K'Ehleyr returned to the Enterprise with her son, Alexander (Jon Steuer, later played by Brian Bonsall), whom she finally admits is also Worf's child.

When K'Ehlfeyr was murdered, Worf placed the boy in the care of his human parents. Worf's Klingon parents were killed by Romulans at the Khitomer Massacre when he was six years of age. He was adopted by the Starfleet officer who found him under the body of his dead mother.

Sergey (Theodore Bikel) and Helena Rozhenko (Georgia Brown), Worf's human parents, who had visited him aboard the Enterprise in "Family," were happy to care for the boy. However, Alexander, grieving for his mother, and longing to be with his father, became withdrawn and unmanageable. Unable to cope with the child, Helena returned him to the Enterprise. Worf, the warrior, was forced to enter the haphazard life of a single parent.

Reunions

Worf was also shocked to learn he had a younger Klingon brother, Kurn (Tony Todd), who was not at Khitomer when their parents died. Kurn became a continuing character and the two brothers joined forces to help end the civil war in the Klingon Empire.

One bond that continues to endure is the marriage of Keiko Ishikawa (Rosalind Chao) and Lieutenant Miles O'Brien (Colm Meaney). Not only was this the first Star Trek wedding, but the only one to date. The couple later had a daughter, Molly, and when O'Brien was offered a promotion, the family transferred to *Deep Space Nine*.

As the series progressed, Data's father, his evil brother Lore (both played by Brent Spiner) and his mother, Juliana Soong (Fionnula Flanagan) have all been introduced. After Lore tried to destroy the Federation, Data was forced to dismantle his brother. In the seventh season episode "Inheritance," Data learns that his mother, unknown to her, is also an android.

Data's great desire to be human leads him to create a daughter (Hallie Todd) in "The Offspring." He names her Lal.

Unfortunately her programming was so advanced that, unlike Data, she developed emotions and could not stand the stress. Despite Data's valiant efforts to correct the problem, she did not survive.

Life on a Starship

The android's efforts to have a normal human relationship first involved a seduction by Tasha Yar (Denise Crosby), in "The Naked Now," which she later denied. During the fourth season's "In Theory," lonely Ensign Janna E'Sora (Michele Scarabelli), pursued Data. He explained that he was not capable of emotional love. This suited Janna for she has been hurt too often by human men. She craved companionship and believed that with Data she would not suffer the pain of broken human relationships. She soon learned that she did, after all, need emotion in

her life and they ceased to be a couple.

Commander LaForge was the last of the crew to have his family explored. His mother, Captain LaForge, is missing along with her ship, the Hera. Geordi soon begins to see/hear images of her, calling to him to save her. The fate of his mother's ship remains a mystery, but he did receive a message from his father (Ben Vereen) who mentioned Geordi's sister, Arianna.

The most mysterious member of the Enterprise crew is Guinan (Whoopi Goldberg). We know only that she is very old, that her world and the majority of her people were destroyed by the Borg. How this happened is also a mystery, as is her past relationship with Picard—a subject neither one will discuss.

Deep Space Relations

*D*eep *Space Nine* is only half way through its second season but already some interesting relationships have developed.

Commanding Officer Benjamin Sisko is a widower with a teenage son, Jake (Cirroc Lofton). While the two have a good rapport, Sisko is learning, as parents have learned since time immemorial, that offspring have minds of their own.

As for Jake, his best friend is Nog, the nephew of the Ferengi bar owner, Quark. Both boys have progressed from playing pranks and watching ships come through the wormhole, to watching girls.

Perhaps more intriguing is Sisko's kinship with Dax (Terry Farrell). She is a Trill, a joined species, and the sixth host for the ancient symbiont named Dax. Sisko first met Dax while a cadet at the Academy— in the body of a fun-loving man, Curzon Dax. Their association covered many years, and memories of some of their exploits were not the kind Sisko would normally share with a woman. Therefore Sisko is having a bit of a problem becoming accustomed to the female version of Dax.

Dr. Julian Bashir (Siddig El Fadil) doesn't see Dax's female form as a problem. Quite the opposite, he finds it a beautiful asset as he attempts to date her (possibly 'court' better describes his actions). All Dax wants is to be good friends.

Kira and Quark

Major Kira has little room in her emotional life for anything, or anyone, but her desire to restore independence for her people and her world. However, when The Ring instituted an insurrection in "The Circle," and Kira took refuge at the monastery, she was amazed to learn that Vadek Beriel (Philip Anglim), one of the religious leaders, was attracted to her. She was even more astonished to realize that the attraction was mutual—a fact she denied when Beriel questioned her, although a vision she experienced through an orb indicated a possible future romance between them.

None of Kira's family members have been introduced.

Chief O'Brien and Keiko's marriage remains a happy one, despite the inconveniences and hardships of the space station.

Quark has a brother, Rom, whom he harasses, cheats, and browbeats. Unadmitted by Quark, his best friend is Odo, whom he shares a love/hate adversarial affinity. Both were present on the space station long before the Federation arrived, and they understand each other.

Cirroc Lofton at Universal Studios. November 13, 1993.
Photo c 1994 Alvert L. Ortega

Quark also has an eye for the ladies, and isn't above entertaining them in a holosuite. But, as with all Ferengi, his real love is profit.

Odo and O'Brien

Odo is a loner, not because he wants to be, but because as a shape-shifter he is one of a kind. Like Quark, Odo would never admit to a friendship with the Ferengi. He is not interested in 'coupling'—was appalled when, on a visit to the space station by Lwaxana Troi, he realized she was attracted to him. After the pair were stranded in a malfunctioning elevator and shared some very poignant moments, the encounter left his mental state in what could only be described as confused. But he also realized that Lwaxana was much more than she seemed. They parted as friends.

Family, friends, lovers—people who are a continuing part of the series, add a new dimension to the adventure. We see Chief O'Brien torn between duty and love for his family when the station must be evacuated. During the same crisis in "The Siege," Nog and Jake worry if they will ever see each other again.

Rick Berman, Michael Piller, and the many writers and producers, have expanded on Roddenberry's vision and given the viewers a show that, in many instances, presents events with which they can identify—similar events that have been a part of their own lives.

A third Star Trek *comic book appeared in 1993. It has resulted in some very interesting stories being published.*

DEEP SPACE NINE: THE COMIC BOOK
by James Van Hise

While DC Comics has had the license to produce *Star Trek* comics for the better part of the last decade, they were actually outbid on the license for a tie-in book with *Deep Space Nine*. A lot of people were surprised by this turn of events, not the least of whom was DC Comics. With a third *Star Trek* title in their roster they could have produced crossover stories like the television series has already done. But with two competing publishers producing *Star Trek* comic books now, that likelihood is reduced.

The good news is that in spite of another publisher producing the latest comic book tie-in, the results are very interesting. In fact Mike Barr, who has written many of the *Star Trek* comic book stories for DC is at the helm of Malibu Comics' *Deep Space Nine*. So Malibu isn't exactly trying to stray far from the tried and true.

In describing the series and his approach to the comic book, Mike Barr stated, "As the producers of the show have said, in the other *Star Trek* shows what they're doing is boldly going where no one has gone before. In that sense, space is the final frontier, as

Gene Roddenberry said. In *Deep Space Nine*, it's kind of a frontier town. If *Star Trek* is the 'wagon train to the stars,' then *Deep Space Nine* is like the frontier town where they stock up before going to that frontier. Frontier towns are always interesting places. They're kind of rough and crude and have a lot of really interesting characters. That's the challenge of *Deep Space Nine*, to tell a number of stories without having the convenient device of having the ship go to a different planet every week."

If there's any problem with the comic book, it is that it suffers from the same limitations which have plagued the television series from the beginning—stories set inside the space station which are more concerned with menacing the main characters than in exploring who the main characters are. The best *Deep Space Nine* television episodes are

those which have illuminated the characters in some manner (i.e. "Emissary" and "Duet") and the weakest have been the menace-of-the-week stories, although the latter are clearly easier to write.

The History of Comics

Let's get something out of the way. Some people disdain the comic book tie-ins to TV shows simply because of what they are called—"Comic books." This is an unfortunate catch-all phrase which was attached to the form almost since its inception in the 1930's. This is because the newspaper strips, which predated comic books, were called "the funnies" since many of them were humor strips. The first reprints of these in the size common to most comic books today were then called "comic books" and the name stuck even when horror, science fic-

tion and super heroes quickly began to dominate the form. But they were all aimed at kids anyway back then, so why not call them comic books?

The first problem with this occurred in the late 1940's when some publishers began producing horror and crime comics which were clearly aimed at older teenagers, and some adults, and yet were available on the magazine racks right alongside *Superman* and *Donald Duck*. There were even Senate hearings into the crime comic books and their effects on children in the 1950's. The result was an industry instituted code of self-regulation which effectively squeezed out any attempts to do more mature material for many years.

As a result comic books didn't have the opportunity to experiment with other kinds of stories until independent publishers emerged

in the '70s, but by then the damage had been done. So far as the American public was concerned, comics were for kids, just as the name implied, and attempts to do adult material have often been regarded as something subversive and have not received widespread ac-ceptance in the United States.

Unlike paperbacks, which are aimed at all types of readers, comics are consistently ignored by most adults and as a result many comic book publishers are resistant to appealing to that large part of the market which won't even give them a second glance. Thus while comic books in Europe are often read by the same reading public who supports bestsellers and other kinds of books, the United States marketplace is very different. Part of this is also caused by the fact that super heroes have long dominated the American comic book.

This has created a self-limiting industry since adults would have little interest in reading about long underwear heroes (even those who avidly went to theaters to see *Batman* in 1989). Attempts to broaden the market to include westerns, mysteries and the like have consistently failed since American western fans and mystery fans look down on the comic book as a form. Thus the industry in North America has remained largely the province of the superhero.

A Well-Crafted TV Tie-In

Occasionally there are diversions, but as with *Deep Space Nine*, they generally come about as a tie-in to a successful movie or a TV show. Just as *Star Trek* fans read new novels based on that series premise, so do some of them give the comic books a try—

enough of them to make a comic book at least moderately successful by publishing standards.

Enter *Deep Space Nine*, and its first five issues which we'll examine here.

"Stowaway" occupies the first two issues if the Malibu comic book and opens with a strange double-age shot of the space station and the wormhole in which the wormhole looks like it's exploding. For some reason artist Gordon Purcell and inker Terry Pallot find it difficult duplicating the special effect seen on screen each and every week at the beginning of the series.

As nice as the rest of the artwork is otherwise, this makes for a rather jarring introduction to the comic book series. But other than this I have no complaints about the art. Purcell's pencils and Pallot's inks are smooth and refined, with none of the rough edges and sloppy inking which have

consistently plagued the movie/TV related comic books of Marvel . Malibu has achieved a slick, polished look to the book which can only serve to attract anyone who picks it up and pages through it.

The likenesses of the characters also survive intact. Since this is accomplished by using photo swipes, it sometimes results in a posed look to some of the characters. But Purcell avoids this as often as not, particularly on page five of issue one in which the Ferengi boy Nog is given some character scenes and interesting facial expressions. What's most remarkable about this is that a variety of facial expressions tend to be the weak point in most comic art, a facet which shows up most vividly when an artist is required to draw real human beings as opposed to the bizarre, semi-human musculature of superheroes with

all of the accompanying twists and impossible poses. Strip that away and you can see how well an artist can really draw when he's commanded to make ordinary humans look interesting. Purcell and Pallot pass that test amazingly well.

Blond Frankenstein

Speaking of real human beings, a supporting character in the story is based on the likeness of John Tesh, the frequent co-host of *Entertainment Tonight*. While they admit to that in the second issue and reveal that it was done with his permission, why they chose him remains unexplained. Did they meet him when they visited Paramount Studios? They don't say. They don't even mention that John Tesh is a *Star Trek* fan and played a Klingon on an episode of *Next Generation*, so there no doubt is a very good reason which they overlook letting the reader in on.

As a result I'm sure that many readers are left thinking—John Tesh? The man Howard Stern calls "blond Frankenstein"? They would have been better off not even pointing out that they used his likeness if they weren't going to explain why they went to all that trouble of including it.

The story is only okay but in fact is at least as good as several plots which have actually appeared on the TV series. It opens with Jake and Nog visiting the science lab of Deep Space Nine with Keiko O'Bri-en's class. What isn't explained is why Nog is there. As established on the TV show, Nog has been forbidden to attend the class by his father, Rom, because of criticism from the Nagus. Jake tutors Nog secretly, so perhaps this story takes place before events seen in the episode "The Nagus."

Anyway, Jake and Nog get into a minor scrape in the lab and later are fooling around down on level 14 when they somehow release a strange organic fungus which turns out to be a threat to the space station. A way to combat it seems impossible to find and even the Cardassians show up wanting to remove the fungus from the station and take it away, leading to the conclusion that this was a failed weapon of theirs which they left behind.

But now that it has become activated somehow, they want to add it to their arsenal, which is exactly why Commander Sisko doesn't want them to have it. The Cardassian who shows up offering his "assistance" is none other than Gul Dukat, who has become something of a semi-regular on the TV series.

Jerome Moore's cover for *Deep Space Nine #6.* "That's the one frustrating angle about working on these books. You have to get all the approval from Paramount, so there's a lot of checks and balances in it"

Inside Deep Space Nine

There's a lot of running around and valiant but futile efforts to defeat the fungus until Jake Sisko admits that he and Nog accidentally let it out, which leads to the reason for the mold's rapid growth and how it can be decimated. It's a very routine story and not a particularly exciting one, but it is on the level of an average episode of the television series, which is the problem.

On the TV show, the wormhole and its path to the Gamma Quadrant hang there like a huge unfulfilled promise. People and things come from the wormhole to Deep Space Nine but only rarely does anyone from DS9 enter the wormhole to do any exploring. With the sole exceptions of "Duet" and "Necessary Evil," the best episodes of *Deep Space Nine* have been those which explored what lies beyond the wormhole, such as in "Battle Lines."

Only so much can be accomplished in a story set on the space station and those built in limitations have never been more evident than in "Stowaway." It's a textbook case of how little can be accomplished in the space station setting as established in this series.

What the TV series claims is that the station can hold seven thousand people (see "Sanctuary"), but nothing has been shown which has given any sense of how vast such a station must be if it can hold that many people. Due to its nature, this station would have no "day" or "night" and as a result would be a constant hub of activity, but we seldom see many people gathered in one place except in extreme situations. Crowds should be the rule rather than the exception on this station since it is situated at the

Early version of Jerome Moore's cover for issue 1 of the Deep Space 9 comic.

gateway to the only known stable wormhole in the galaxy.

If the TV show doesn't have the budget for such crowd scenes on the Promenade and elsewhere, certainly the comic book would where the visuals are limited only by the artist's ability and imagination, and Gordon Purcell is far better than your average comic book artist.

Drawing Deep Space Nine

Purcell is the pencil artist in four of the first five issues and was interviewed for a special *Deep Space Nine* giveaway item packaged with the first issue of *Hero* magazine. There the artist talked about how he transforms a script into a story.

"I break it down a couple of times," the artist explained. "I read the script once, to get an idea of what's going on and to see if I need any reference material. I'm trying to videotape all the episodes of the TV show, so if I'm aware that there's something I need to see, I can watch the tape again. After that, I look through the script again and do thumbnails with stick figures, so I know what the flow of action is. Then I usually go to the regular paper board. I like to make sure it reads well from left to right and has something strong on each page."

Purcell had previously drawn *Star Trek* comic books for D.C. and had three years experience doing that before being approached to draw *Deep Space Nine*.

Issue three features the story "Old Wounds" written by Mike W. Barr and drawn by Rob Davis and Terry Pallott (although Gordon Pur-cell is erroneously credited on the front cover). Just as with issue one, the front cover is a very nicely rendered scene by Jerome Moore (with color added by Rochard Ory). Jerome has done

many covers for the DC *Star Trek* titles and to have him do some *Deep Space Nine* covers continues a winning combination.

The Art of Jerome Moore

Unlike some artists, Jerome does more than just try to capture the likenesses of the characters he renders for the *Star Trek* comics. He also strives to create an artistically interesting scene. Compare Jerome's covers on *Deep Space Nine* #'s 1 & 3 with the covers by others artists on issues 2, 4 & 5. Jerome brings a solid sense of design and artistic sensibility to his renderings which are missing from the other covers. All too often the artists of TV and movie tie-in comics think that if they get the likenesses down well, they've done their job. This overlooks the fact that the scene should be an interesting design in and of itself apart from who is being portrayed. Jerome consistently delivers on this.

Jerome described to me how he became involved with the *Deep Space Nine* comic book, stating, "Once I found out that Malibu was going to be doing DS9 (which D.C. didn't like too much), I was asked to do the first issue's cover. I've gotten a name for myself doing *Star Trek* covers now," Jerome explained. "I've been in the business a long time, but when I really made my mark it was doing the *Star Trek* covers."

In describing his approach to drawing covers, Jerome stated, "What I mostly do is portraiture, similar to what Keith Birdsong does on the novels." Jerome takes a different approach than just trying to translate it into comic book action, which Marvel did, and D.C. did a long time before he got on the book. "Likenesses were not really stressed, but with me I wanted to go more towards movie poster design, inspired by Drew Struzan. He's done *Star Wars* posters, Indiana Jones and book jacket work. So I had more of an influence where I'm going to nail the likenesses. That's what people buy it for. That's going to jump out at you on the stands.

"I don't want to compete with Spider-Man and X-Men where the action is just over the top, and I don't think *Star Trek* should try to compete with them," Jerome adds. "I wanted to go the other way and do things a little bit more subtle that draw you in. You'll walk by the comic book rack and you'll look and see all the stuff just glaring at you and screaming for attention, and *Star Trek* will stand out on its own by doing something totally different."

Conceiving a Cover Design

The way Jerome conceives a cover begins with the script which he reads and then picks an interesting key scene which he tries to portray on the cover. He draws a sketch of this which must be approved by Paramount before he can draw the finished version.

"That's the one frustrating angle about working on these books. You have to get all the approval from Paramount, so there's a lot of checks and balances in it," Jerome explained. "With the first DS9 cover I had to change a couple things. They want Dax pretty much to remain not really sexual; they don't want her to portray any kind of sexuality. She's a beautiful woman but I had her hair in a ponytail draped over her shoulder on the first issue's cover and they said, 'We don't want any feminine flourish in her

hair.' They want Dax to be an alluring character but not over the top sexually. I didn't think that was over the top, so I don't always agree with the changes."

Also on the cover of *Deep Space Nine* #1, Jerome Moore had Major Kira holding up a phaser and even though there wasn't anything overtly violent about the pose, the phaser had to be removed.

"Sometimes they'll be arbitrary about certain things just to maintain Gene Roddenberry's image of *Star Trek* being this peaceful non-*Star Wars* type of universe. Now and then I come across where Paramount draws the line. Malibu had a great start with that first issue. It got a lot of attention. They did it really well. I think their first issue is the best debut for a *Star Trek* title in co-

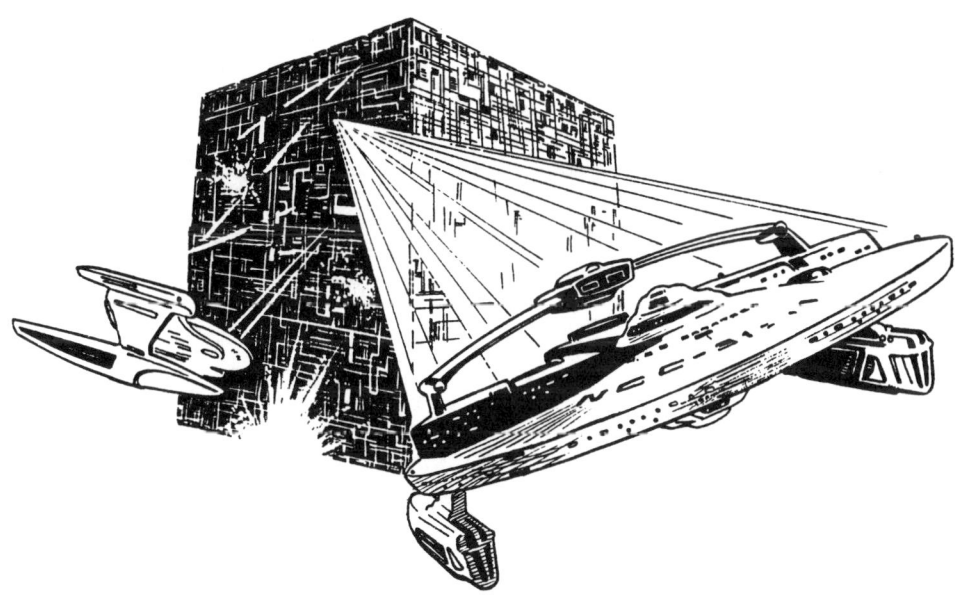

"I prefer the whole Star Trek credo of going out where no man has gone before." Instead of to boldly sit where no one has sat before, as some have observed about Deep Space Nine" explains artist Jerome Moore.

mics that was ever done. All the way through the quality was up.

Hotel in Space

"The cover was a combination of a painting style plus the standard black and white, which is what I usually do. They did a blueline on that. Gold Key did paintings and they did photo covers, but they didn't really meld the two. Malibu pretty much covered all the bases. They did a photo cover, a blue line which was a painting and they really had a good jumping off point. It remains to be seen whether or not they are going to be able to maintain any kind of quality. I'm still doing an occasional cover for them. I've done three already, and inked one and hope to do some more for them."

Regarding the characters on this new version of *Star Trek*, Jerome has some specific observa-tions relating to the series itself.

"I like Sisko, but he has a lot of potential that's not being tapped yet. Odo is interesting. He's like the Data type; the Spock type character that has a lot of secrets behind him that you want to explore. I like Kira, mainly because she is more like a defacto Ensign Ro. It's just the dark nature of it, like being trapped on that station and the religious undertones of the Bajorans is what I think is hamstringing it. I prefer the whole *Star Trek* credo of going out where no man has gone before." Instead of to boldly sit where no one has sat before, as some have observed about *Deep Space Nine*.

"I've heard someone say that it's like *Hotel* in space. We're not really getting to see too much of the Gamma Quadrant, but it's still young, so you have to give it a chance."

The Cardassian Question

Writer Mike Barr delivers an above par *Deep Space Nine* story in "Old Wounds" which tells the tale of Gul Trelar, a Cardassian known as the "Butcher of Bajor" who wants to return to Bajor because it was the world of his birth. This sets up a paradox. Barr draws from the *Deep Space Nine* writer's guide in crafting the idea behind this story as that guide stipulates that the Cardassians controlled Bajor for one hundred years.

Unfortunately this is contradicted by the *Next Generation* episode "Ensign Ro" which introduced the Bajorans. Ensign Ro clearly states in that episode that the Bajorans have been suffering under Cardassian subjugation for forty years. To try to change that later is a bit too late unless they were to go back and redub the dialogue in that *Next Generation* episode. To confuse matters even more, the episode "Sanctuary" in the second season of *Deep Space Nine* states that the Cardassians were on Bajor for fifty years.

According to the storyline of "Old Wounds," Gul Trelar and his family are coming to the space station because this is as close as the Bajorans will allow him to get to their world. Commander Sisko is ordered to go along with this, apparently for political reasons. Because of Kira Nerys background as a Bajoran terrorist battling the Cardassian rule, this becomes her story, particularly since she once had a run-in with Gul Trelar who murdered another Bajoran right before her eyes.

This flashback scene is odd as the reason Gul Trelar killed the Bajoran is arbitrary and even though Kira attacked the Cardassian physically, whether she's punished for this is never revealed.

A preliminary Deep Space Nine sketch by Jerome Moore.

She hates the Cardassian for being a murderer but realistically one would have thought that Gul Trelar would have made her life a living hell for daring to attack him. If he did, we're never told about it.

An interesting twist in the story is that the Cardassian's current wife is not only Bajoran, but one of those who actually witnessed Gul Trelar's murder of another Bajoran in the presence of Kira Nerys. Although she ex-plains that he freed her parents in exchange for accepting his companionship, this aspect isn't adequately explored. The reason for this is apparently because the story is complete in one issue whereas a two issue storyline would have featured more room for character

development of the supporting characters.

Future Crime

When Gul Trelar is murdered in a holosuite and there's no record of anyone entering it to commit the crime, the writer makes the same sort of mistake here as the writers on the TV show often make. They write a story set in the future but don't allow the characters to think the way that someone in the future would think. In the absence of any actual suspects, checking the holosuite programming would have been the first thing they would have done. Instead it's practically the last thing they think of, and then only after the killer attempts to cover his tracks by damaging the holosuite.

So for both good and bad reasons, "Old Wounds" is exactly the sort of *Deep Space Nine* story you could expect to

have seen on the TV series.

The cover of *Deep Space Nine* #3 is drawn by Jerome Moore and the approach taken to it was inspired by the shattering special effect seen in the *Next Generation* episode "Frame Of Mind."

"Odo is supposed to solve a murder mystery so I have all these puzzle pieces floating around him," Jerome explained in describing his inspiration behind the image he rendered. "The suspects are those who are involved and their faces are on the puzzle pieces floating around him. And in the back there is this overall image of the Cardassian that was murdered and his image is actually the puzzle; it's just shattering and spinning around Odo."

Questioning the Prime Directive

Issues 4 & 5 feature the two part story "Emancipation" by Mike W. Barr,

Gordon Purcell and Terry Pallot. This reads like something we'd expect to see on *Deep Space Nine* next week and beat for beat is exactly the style of the stories seen on the TV show. And since it's a two part story it is able to develop certain aspects of the plot and character which would come up short in a one issue storyline.

The story opens with Dr. Bashir and Dax in a runabout in the Gamma Quadrant where they had been doing some exploring down on a planet where they'd found a plant which bloomed in the dark. But then they encounter a large spacecraft. Recognizing that the technology is inferior to their own, they allow themselves to be drawn aboard with a tractor beam in order to discover the intentions of these beings.

Once each side begins to trust the other and Julian tends to their medical needs, they guide the vessel to the wormhole and to Deep Space Nine. There the leader of the aliens, Mardak, requests asylum for his people as they are fleeing a race of oppressors. Sisko explains that he has to take that up with his superiors, which is the first clue that this will become a story involving the Prime Directive.

The Prime Directive is supposed to allow races to develop naturally without interference from the Federation, but occasionally loopholes seem to appear. For instance, in the *Next Generation* episode "Homeward," Captain Picard is perfectly willing to allow the people on a planet to die out when a natural phenomenon is destroying their atmosphere, even though it is within his power to save them.

Isn't there a line to be drawn between non-interference and neglect? Between benign neglect

and manslaughter? How about allowing a race of people to live as slaves? This is exactly the question raised in "Emancipation."

When Commander Sisko discovers that the aliens are fleeing from a culture that practices slavery, he must decide whether the Prime Directive applies since slavery is a normal part of that culture. Major Kira can't begin to understand how the Federation could consider returning a people into slavery, and seeing Ben Sisko, a black man, discussing the situation as though it's a legal abstraction is very strange indeed.

The Nature of Chiaran Slavery

Sisko's race never seems to enter into any of the *Deep Space Nine* stories, either on the TV show or in the comic book. Even in this story there is no scene in which Sisko considers the kind of lives his ancestors might have endured five hundred years before. Even if his ancestors were from Africa rather than from the United States, African nations enslaved members of rival tribes and those captured in war well into the 19th century. In fact the slave trade with Europe and North America flourished largely because of African tribes selling their enemies to the representatives of other continents. But nothing touching on the issue is never raised in the story as it concentrates on how the escaped slaves deal with both freedom and the prospect of recapture.

Soon a second ship arrives at the space station, this one commanded by Rogon. Although the slaves escaped from his world, he's willing to negotiate the situation with Sisko. In spite of being a slavemaster, Rogon is portrayed as being understanding and willing to compromise. Complicating the situation is that Mardak's mother is Rogon's personal slave and she accepts her station in life.

The nature of how some Chiarans become slaves as opposed to being of the ruling class isn't revealed. The slaves have a scarlet jewel embedded in their foreheads, but other than this they look the same as their masters, so the subjugation is apparently not racial. Whether it is religious or ancestral is not revealed either.

What is explored is how the former slaves react to freedom and the fact that some of them are clearly incapable of dealing with it. One of them even states that he doesn't like being free. Mardak doesn't want to take the chance that they'll be sent back, and so he tries to destroy the wormhole. When that fails a bomb is set off in

Quark's place, resulting in the death of Mardak's mother. Whether Mardak is the one who set off the bomb remains unclear, although if it was he who caused his mother's death, that would be particularly grim and ironic.

Stories With Substance

An interesting twist is thrown in when Rogon agrees to grant the slaves their unqualified freedom, while also allowing those to return with him who wish to do so. As a result Rogon's lieutenants mutiny and attack the station, trying to take the slaves back by force in order to insure that there are no uprisings on the homeworld when other slaves there learn that some of their fellows successfully found freedom.

When everything is resolved, the result is an unusual and interesting story which is actually about something. The best episodes of *Deep*

Space Nine have thus far been about something. "Duet" dealt with war crimes and the guilt experienced by those who may have participated in them. "In The Hands Of The Prophets" was almost about religious intolerance, but then turned out to be about something entirely different.

What the *Deep Space Nine* comic book has managed to do is capture the style of the television series in that it tells different kinds of stories and seems to be exploring them from just as many different angles as the television show has done, while also employing the same sort of, well, shall we say "creative restraint" that the TV series sometimes suffers from.

There's a whole wide galaxy out there beyond the wormhole and eventually fans are going to get tired of sitting back and waiting for the inhabitants to come to Deep Space Nine when Sisko and company are fully capable of going out there themselves. It would be good if the comic book could indulge in some of this as well, unless Para-mount is holding them back.

What is writer Mike Barr's approach? In an interview in *The Malibu Sun #1*, a previews publication published by Malibu Comics in March 1993, Barr stated, "If we've done our job well, the ideal compliment I could get from this would be to get a letter from some reader who said, 'I didn't care about watching the *Deep Space Nine* TV show, until I read the comic, and I thought I'd give it a try.' I think if we can do a good comic book that brings together all the aspects of *Deep Space Nine*, and stands on its own as a comic book, then I'll be really happy."

 ***Deep Space Nine: The Comic Book***

Avery Brooks, Rene Auberjonois and Sadig El Fadil at Universal Studios, November 13, 1993.
Photo c 1994 Chris Flicker

Would human beings in the 24th century be as peaceful and under-standing as Gene Roddenberry liked to hope, or does life on Deep Space Nine *actually cut closer to reality than* The Next Generation *does?*

CONFLICT ON STAR TREK
by Kay Doty

By the time Gene Roddenberry sat down to write his "Wagon Train to the Stars" series, he had served many years as both a military and a police officer. It is very probable that he'd seen enough conflict to last several lifetimes. Ever the optimist, Roddenberry envisioned a world free of conflict. A universe populated with people who were congenial and friendly with each other. That was the way he wrote.

But the cold hard facts are that conflict has been around since the beginning of time and is not likely to end by the twenty-third or twenty-fourth centuries—unless, of course, the Organian Council becomes active again.

AN EXPLORER, NOT A FIGHTER

Roddenberry always insisted that the Enterprise was an explorer or science vessel, not a warship. Any battles would be fought in self-defense, but never, never would Starfleet or the Federation be the instigator! This concept has endured through four series (including the animated episodes), six movies and over a hundred novels written by professional writers.

He carried this concept even further. There would be no friction between crew members. Of course there was the on-going love/hate feud between Spock and McCoy, but they were seldom really mad at each other. Besides it was entertaining for a crew who often went months, even years, between shore leaves; and the fans loved the verbal combat.

"Where No Man Has Gone Before" portrayed Kirk as angry at Mr. Spock, his inherited first officer, when the Vulcan suggested that Gary Mitchell must be killed before it became too late.

Occasionally a crew member stepped out of line, or didn't do his job properly and Kirk (and infrequently Spock) spoke sharply or reprimanded the offender, but that was their jobs, and these occurrences were rare. Then there was Dr. McCoy, who never quite knew, or cared, where the line lay between critical advice and insubordination. His captain was forced to point out this distinction to the good doctor from time to time.

McCoy was prone to snap at a medic or nurse when they didn't move fast enough to suit him, but these were isolated events, and no outright dislike existed among crew members.

PEOPLE UNDER PRESSURE

This same theory carried over into the *Next Generation* crew to an even greater degree. All crew members are close friends. Angry words might be uttered in the heat of battle or a life threatening crisis, then later forgotten. Aliens sometimes appropriated the bodies and/or minds of some crew members for their own purposes, as in "Power Play," "The Game," "Future Imper-

Rene Auberjonois at Sony Studios for the State Summer School for the Arts press conference.
Photo c 1994 Alvert L. Ortega

fect," "Hollow Pursuits," forcing them to act in a manner foreign to their normal personalities, but once the alien entity was expelled, the crew members returned to their conventional selves.

During the second season a Spock/McCoy type relationship was attempted between Dr. Pulaski (Diana Muldaur) and Data. That didn't work. Perhaps the chem-istry was wrong between the two actors, or enough time wasn't available to allow the wrangling to develop naturally. Had Muldaur remained with the series the rivalry might have taken on a life of its own. Another problem came from some fans who did-n't like to see Data "picked on."

When Rick Berman and Michael Piller began planning *Deep Space Nine*

John Glover, guest star on episode "Invasive Procedures", at the Westwood Marquis 3rd Annual reception for Emmy Nominees.
Photo c 1994 Alvert L. Ortega

Roddenberry knew about the proposed new series, but was ill and had little input into the show's direction. One report even claims that Roddenberry didn't like the idea and was opposed to it. The fact that *Deep Space Nine* was not announced as being in development until several weeks after Roddenberry's death lends some credence to this rumor.

With *Deep Space Nine*, Berman and Piller sought to induce a more realistic work environment. The station was located at the far reaches of space. Beings from a variety of worlds, races, and species would be living and working there, each with differing cultures and opinions of what constituted right and wrong. It would be unreasonable to expect them all to like and admire each other.

Life Aboard Deep Space Nine

Try picturing Major Kira sitting down for a pleasant game of poker with Quark, or Chief O'Brien sipping tea with Dr. Bashir while chatting about the latest show on the entertainment channel. Not hardly!

When Starfleet arrived at *Deep Space Nine*, the station was a mess. It had been vandalized by the departing Cardassians. Few things worked and those that did soon malfunctioned, bringing a continual scowl to the face of the usually jovial Chief of Operations, Miles O'Bri-en.

After the departure of the Cardassians, Major Kira was furious when the Federation and Starfleet were invited by her government to administer *Deep Space Nine*. She believed the station should be run by Bajorans for Bajorans. Furious, she directed her wrath at Sisco.

Kira was convinced that she would be better qualified to make decisions about Bajor than Sisco. When he disagreed with what she believed to be the correct course of action, she was resentful that, as his second-in-command of the station, she had to take orders from a Starfleet officer. In her more rational moments she is fully aware that, with many factions in the Bajoran government at each others throats, her world just might collapse without the Federation.

A Clash of Personalities

Many of the discussions between Commander Sisko and his first officer are heated, but they have learned to respect each other. Kira is like a powder keg waiting to be ignited, and Sisko is aware that he must be vigilant—ready to confiscate her

matches, so to speak.

In addition, Sisko understands Kira's passion for her homeland, and is willing to direct, what others might consider insubordination, into positive channels.

Had Kira been assigned to the Enterprise as first officer under either Kirk or Picard, she would have enjoyed a very brief tenure—neither captain would have tolerated such insubordination, but Sisko understands the passion that drives her and can be forgiving when she oversteps her position.

Sisko himself was less than happy at being ordered to take command of *Deep Space Nine*, and planned to leave as soon as a replacement could be found. However, circumstances, and the challenge, changed his mind. His low-key style of command contrasts with the turmoil surrounding him, earning him the respect of his

Chris Sarandon, guest star in "Rivals" at an Avco Cinema premiere.
Photo c 1994 Alvert L. Ortega

officers and the station's residents.

Dr. Bashir earned the disdain of both Kira and O'Brien with his naive comments about coming to the frontier for excitement and adventure. They don't actually dis-like him, and in truth respect his medical skills, but believe he has an idyllic view of the station that is far from accurate. Bashir has a cheerful disposition, sometimes ruffling the feelings of others with his

Rene Auberjonois at Universal Studio's Meet the Cast of
Star Trek: Deep Space Nine.   **Photo c 1994 Alvert L. Ortega**

ings of others with his innocent comments.

The Enigma of Odo

Constable Odo is an enigma, to himself as much as to his fellow officers. A shape shifter, he knows nothing of his origins—and is constantly searching for information. He was held up to ridicule and exploited by the Cardassians. A loner, he is snappish with everyone. If pressed, Odo would likely admit that Kira is the closest thing he has to a friend. Both would deny it, but his Spock-McCoy like bickering with Quark is a friendship of sorts. Each has shown concern for the other in times of peril.

Odo has served on the station longer than anyone else and resents anyone who tells him how to do his job, or suggests, by an inadvertent remark, that he might do better.

Dax is the best liked member of the crew—and also the oldest, having lived through at least six hosts and approximately 300 years. Her quiet demeanor and sincere smile can restore some semblance of calm to situations when all around her is chaos.

Quark is the least liked resident of the station. Crew members think of him as a greedy, conniving manipulator—which he is. His greatest conflict is with anyone who might try to separate him from his gold-pressed latinum, or prevent an advantageous deal. But even he has shown (reluctantly) a compassionate side during a crisis.

The Challenge of the Stars

Except for the vast distances, living at the outer reaches of space might be compared to the settling of America. There would be many

Frank Langella, guest star in season 2 premier, at Century Plaza 92 Cable Forum to promote Showtime's "Monkey House" by Kurt Vonnegut.
Photo c 1994 Alvert L. Ortega

problems, many obstacles to overcome in both instances. It seems reasonable to believe people would disagree and make enemies in the twenty-fourth century, just as they did in the seventeenth century.

Poets have written that love makes the world go around—and to a degree that may be true, but conflict, discontent, animosity, and friction also play a role in the human existence. Without it there is no challenge—no reason to go on to bigger and better things. Without challenge mankind would never have looked to the stars or wondered what lay hidden behind the black curtain of space.

Barbara Bosson (guest starred in "Rivals" in the second season of Deep Space Nine*) and Steven Bochco having dinner at Spagos.*
Photo c 1994 Alvert L. Ortega

Without challenge Gene Roddenberry would have had no reason to write *Star Trek*.

The dictionary defines challenge with such words as provoke, threaten, denounce, dare and question—all action words which in most cases would lead to conflict.

To their credit, Berman and Piller have developed a realistic (if that word is appropriate when referring to science fiction) show based on

The entire cast of Deep Space Nine at Universal Studios on November 13, 1993.

Photo c 1994 Chris Flicker

their concept of how people might be living, working, agreeing and disagreeing, three or four hundred years into the future.

Deep Space Nine *introduced something new to the* Star Trek *universe not seen there before—a religious backdrop.*

RELIGION AND TREK
by Kay Doty

A number of *Star Trek* fans have complained of the lack of religion in the *Star Trek* series. There is justification for their complaints. However, in television this is the norm.

Since the advent of television there are/were few continuing dramas with a religious theme. There have been a scattering of shows, such as Michael Landon's *Little House on the Prairie* with characters who do attend church. In *Highway to Heaven*, another Landon series, he played an angel who returned to Earth to help people in trouble. These shows are exceptions.

It isn't unusual, in earth-bound series, for characters to discuss attending church during such religious holidays as Easter, Christmas, or Hanukkah, but otherwise most writers and producers are content to leave TV religion to the ministers, priests, and evangelists. *Star Trek* followed the same format—until *Deep Space Nine* debuted.

As the series begins: Commander Benjamin Sisko had arrived at his new post on the space station less than an hour before he was approached by an elderly monk, who led him to meet the Kai, Bajor's spiritual leader. She was a

middle-aged lady named Opaka, who greeted him warmly.

Opaka tells Sisko of the prophets, that their promise to send an emissary has arrived—in the person of Benjamin Sisko. Although Sisko insists that she is mistaken, Opaka was not to be dissuaded.

Opaka shows him a glowing green orb that she calls "The Tear of the Prophet." Within seconds Sisko is transported into another dimension where he not only meets the prophets but a few ghosts of his own. From that beginning the Bajoran religions have been a reoccurring storyline as the series progresses.

The Fate of Kai Opaka

In "Battle Lines," Opaka pays a surprise visit to the space station and asks to be taken on a tour of the wormhole. Sisko reluctantly does so, accompanied by Kira and Dr. Bashir. Their runabout is pulled off course and crash lands on a moon, killing Opaka.

Miraculously she was revived by a bio-mechanical presence in the atmosphere that prevents death from occurring—however she will die if she leaves. Kira was devastated, but Opaka calmly stated that she was called to this place by the prophets. She explains to Sisko, "My work is here now, Commander. But your path and mine will cross again."

With Opaka gone, a new Kai must be selected. There are many candidates but few who are qualified, and the selection process is slow. One who covets the position openly is Vedek Winn, the leader of small militant sect who believes Bajor should return to the old ways—that all non-Bajorans must leave their world, including from the space station.

*Armin Shimmerman
(Quark) sans makeup at
Universal Studios.
November 13, 1993.*
Photo c 1994 Chris Flicker

Winn disapproved of the Bajoran government's action in asking the Federation to administer the station while Bajor recovered from the devastation left behind by the departing Cardas-sians. The sixty years of harsh Cardassian occupation left the Bajoran Provincial Government officials ineffective, fighting among themselves, and in need of outside help. Once their recovery was complete the ruling ministers hope to gain admission to the Federation. Vedek Winn was adamantly opposed to that.

A Political Plot

Winn came unexpectedly to the space station and interrupted Keiko O'Brien's science class at the school one day (See "In The Hands Of The Prophets"). She accused the teacher of blasphemy for not discussing the prophets' role in the development of the wormhole.

Keiko refused to alter her teachings. She tried to explain that she was teaching science, and it was Winn who should teach about spiritual matters. The Vedek berated Keiko and angri-

Louis Fletcher, guest star on "In the Hands of the Prophets," having dinner at Spagos restaurant.
Photo c 1994 Alvert L. Ortega

ly left the school, saying she would not be responsible for the consequences. Many of the Bajorans took their children out of the school, which was subsequently destroyed by a bomb. Fortunately there were no injuries.

That act of violence prompted Vedek Bereil, next in line to serve as Kai, to go to the station. When an assassination attempt was made on Bereil's life, Sisko suspected Winn. He angrily accused her of creating the trouble to get her fellow Vedek out of the monastery, where one of her followers could kill him. This would leave the door open for her to become the next Kai. Winn simply turned and walked away. There was not, however, any way Sisko could prove his accusations.

That incident was not the end of the problems with Vedek Winn. In the first three episodes of the second season, "The Homecoming," "The Circle" and "The Siege," Winn conspired with Minister Jaro, one of the ministers of the Bajoran Provincial Government, to drive the Federation out of the space station.

They purchased weapons and committed acts of terrorism that included the kidnapping and torture of Major Kira—all in the name of religion. After Kira was rescued by Starfleet officers, she found proof that the weapons were purchased indirectly from the Bajoran's old enemies, the Cardassians. Realizing that their plot had failed, Winn and Jaro do a slick about-face and demand the arrest and conviction of the guilty parties—themselves excluded of course.

Sidetrack But Not Sidelined

Minister Jaro was a political opportunist who wanted to rule Bajor and was willing to go to any lengths to gain his objective.

Vedek Winn was even more dangerous for she will not give up. She devoutly believes that she knows what is best for Bajor. She is the beloved spiritual leader of a small, devoted group of followers who will abide by her teachings. They will obey her orders, citing them as the will of the prophets, as did Neela, the officer who attempted to murder Vedek Bereil.

Commander Sisko is under no illusions that he has seen the last of the determined Vedek Winn.

Holy wars are a continuing part of earth's history. It is reasonable to assume these struggles have also transpired on worlds in outer space. In the original series episode "Balance of Terror," Kirk was in the midst of performing a marriage ceremony for two of his officers, Specialists Robert Tomlinson and Angela Martine, when Romulans attacked. During the battle Tomlinson was killed. Once hostilities ended, Kirk went in search of Martine, finding her in the ship's chapel where he offered her comfort. This was the only time the chapel set was used during the series.

The Next Generation had numerous events that could properly have used an ecclesiastical setting but did not. One of these was the wedding of Keiko Ishikawa and Chief Miles O'Brien, held instead in Ten Forward.

The memorial service for Tasha Yar could better have been held in a chapel than on the holodeck.

Armin Shimmerman at the Belage Hotel for the press conference of "Kiss & Unite" concert to benefit Pediatric AIDS.

Roddenberry and Religion

The powers-that-be who determine a show's content have stated, off the record, that including a religious theme can be dangerous.

With so many denominations in just the United States alone, no matter how well a spiritual plot was written and performed, someone would be offended.

There are many parallels to Vedek Winn in today's society who could very well take offense, if they even recognized themselves. Belief in a supreme being has existed since the beginning of civilization and that belief is not likely to disappear in the next three to four hundred years. Piller and Berman have introduced the delicate subject of religion into the show in a manner that shouldn't be offensive to anyone, but at the same time allows the viewer to assume the show's char-acters have their own personal deity.

But how did Gene Roddenberry himself view religion? It is perhaps because of his own personal outlook, more than any other reason, that *Star Trek* had avoided portraying any sort of religions on a regular basis before *Deep Space Nine*. At the time *Star Trek The Next Generation* was in its early seasons, and about a year before his death, Roddenberry made the following observations.

"I am very concerned, and want to find a way, to get into the fact that

Cast with Producers Rick Berman and Michael Piller.
Photo c 1994 Alvert L. Ortega

most of the warfare and killing going on in the world is going on in the name of religion; organized religion. Not that I'm saying that there are not great plans and that we are not part of some great thing, but it is not the type of thing you see preached on television. I don't hold anyone up to ridicule. My mother is a good Baptist and she believes in many great things. But I cannot sit still in a series of this type and not point out who's killing who in the world."

Men as Gods

Roddenberry did actually oversee an episode questioning religion, "Who Watches The Watchers?" in season three. On a primitive planet, an off world survey team is accidentally discovered by the inhabitants, who come to regard the Enterprise crewmen and their miraculous feats (ap-pearing and disappearing via the transporter beam) as the actions of gods.

"I've always thought that, if we did not have supernatural explanations for all the things we might not understand right away, this is the way we would be, like the people on that planet," Gene explained. "I was born into a supernatural world in which all my people—my family—usually said, 'That is because God willed it,' or gave other supernatural explanations for whatever happened. When you confront those statements on their own, they just don't make sense. They are clearly wrong. You need a certain amount of proof to accept anything, and that proof was not forthcoming to support those statements."

This clash between religion and science was portrayed, to a timorous degree, on the *Deep Space Nine* episode "In The

Hands Of The Prophets," but was done in such a way that any parallels of meaning between the science versus creationism theory debates on earth were quickly sidetracked and dissipated.

The Bajoran religion (which has thus far not even been given a name) continues to slowly unfold in the background. How dynamically it will ultimately take hold on the show remains to be seen.

Science fiction is a realm which asks questions and offers possible solutions. But are all of those solutions thought through as carefully as they might have been?

QUESTIONS ABOUT DEEP SPACE NINE
By Wendy Rathbone

Every once in awhile I just can't help playing devil's advocate when I watch television or movies. Sometimes the characters say and do things that make me think, why that? How could that be? Do they really believe what they're saying? When I watch a horror movie, I often wonder why the victim runs into the deep woods instead of into the crowded shopping mall across the way. When I watch action/adventure movies, I wonder why the heroes stay clean, their injuries (broken bones, etc.) heal so quickly. I wonder: when do they sleep or eat or go to the bathroom?

When I watch science fiction, some of these same questions come to me, but I find it more interesting because science fiction actually tackles the world, twists it inside out and makes me look at things from a different perspective. Then the questions take on more depth.

Continuity Quirks

When I find blunders in plot or character, science fiction, by its very nature, almost always offers me wonderful alternative possibilities. You can endlessly fill in between the lines because science in the future is so advanced as to seem like magic. The dead don't stay dead in science fiction. (Nor do they seem to in soap operas, but that's another article.) The characters on *Deep Space Nine* aren't all human, so their reactions could be termed 'alien' instead of the results of bad acting, bad writing and bad directing.

Still, questions persist. I can't help it. Why can't Data speak in contractions when he is able to mimic contractions and other slang forms of speech when 'acting' or reading? Why do aliens' lips move in synch with the universal translator? Why isn't everything in Kirk's, Spock's, Picard's, Worf's, etc., quarters broken to smithereens after the ship is attacked? Small earthquakes on Earth have been known to do more damage than an all out attack on the ship that leaves fragile vases standing, weapons and pictures still attached to walls, books still neatly stacked on shelves. And my all time favorite STAR TREK question: Why did Khan and Chekov recognize each other in *The Wrath of Khan* when Chekov had not yet been assigned to the Enter-prise in "Space Seed?"

For *Deep Space Nine*, similar questions persist. Perhaps there are just some things I'll never understand and I should accept that. But on the other hand, it's always fun to wonder: Why can't Odo get his features right? He says he looks unformed because he could never quite master the features of the Bajorans who raised him. But he can

Sadig El Fadil at Universal Q&A with Cast.
Photo c 1994 Alvert L. Ortega

Avery Brooks at the Pasadena Civic Center at the 1993 Technical Emmy Awards, as a presenter.
Photo c 1994 Alvert L. Ortega

Colm Meany at the Director's Guild for the premiere of his film "Snapper."

Photo c 1994 Alvert L. Ortega

Cast at Universal Studios.   **Photo c 1994 Alvert L. Ortega**

master quite well the intricate details of the face of a rat or a mouse, the smooth, streamlined effect of a table, or a flashing instrument panel on the wall. Why are Bajoran features so difficult for him? And while we're at it, just what gender is he, really? We don't really know that, either, do we? Did Odo choose the male form because it's more convenient? Does Odo even know what gender he truly is? Is the term "gender" even applicable to a shapeshifter whose natural state is a form-less blob?

Spic and Span

Why, in all the Trek's, and especially *Deep Space Nine*, are people's house-keeping skills so perfect? Not a speck of dust mars Sisko's or Kira's quarters. Quark never has dirty dishes. This is one of those questions where, by reading between the lines, we can assume

advanced technology we never see helps out a lot. But still, someone has to mop and polish the floors, don't they? (I remember, much to my amazement, seeing someone doing just that in the background of one of the scenes in *The Wrath of Khan*. I was most impressed.)

Why does the alien makeup on *Deep Space Nine* get more and more elaborate? Is alien-in-appearance all that counts? What about alien culture, behavior and belief? You can have alien humans, but I guess that's too subtle for Hollywood. In one *Deep Space Nine* episode, I remember an alien with skin flaps that attached his nose to his chin, making it very difficult for him to speak. How does he eat? How does he kiss? Who is responsible for this ridiculous makeup design? If he had flaps that detached, why, then I might understand. Or if his mouth

Sadig El Fadil at Universal Q&A with cast.
Photo c 1994 Alvert L. Ortega

were in a different spot.

On a similar note, why do they try to make the aliens as ugly as possible? I know ugly is in the eye of the beholder and all that, but wouldn't there, by virtue of diversity, be pretty aliens as well? (And I mean other than love interests for Sisko and Bashir.) I'm not saying all the aliens are ugly, just 90 percent. There have been some most attractive Bajoran men, I might add. Still, I can't help believing the ugly alien syndrome is

simply a ploy to outdo last week's alien shock.

Quark's Place

Why isn't Quark rich beyond his wildest dreams by now? He does well with all the aliens that pass through *Deep Space Nine*. Is he a terrible businessman? Or is he a miser who can never have enough?

Why are there only Dabo girls in Quark's casino/bar? Why no Dabo men? Dabo neuters?

Why aren't the holo-suites booked up for the next 100 years? Are they extremely expensive to use? (For that matter, I never understood why there weren't long lines outside the free Enterprise holodeck rooms on *Next Generation*. What a grand invention. They'd have to sell tickets, I'd think, to accommodate everyone fairly.)

Just how, exactly, does that universal translator work? If it's a brain implant, does it translate, or teach? If it isn't telepathic and able to teach Federation Standard instantly to new races, then why, when aliens speak, don't their lips move out of synch with the words we hear? In the episode "Sanctuary" we got to see the Universal Translator at work, but when the aliens stopped speaking their own tongue and were suddenly speaking Federation standard English, it lost me as the explanation for how it accomplished that feat was never forthcoming.

Questions, questions, questions. Maybe future episodes of *Deep Space Nine* will supply a few of the answers.

A DEEP SPACE NINE GLOSSARY
By Michael Ruff

This glossary of names and terms used in the first season of DEEP SPACE NINE covers all 19 episodes in the first season and lists the episode in which the name or term first appeared listed in parenthesis.

A

AHB-JADAH
Egg-like decoration stolen from a Vanoben Transport ship, and offered by the twin Miradorns to Quark for 1000 bars of gold-pressed latinum. ("Vortex")

AH-KEL
(Randy Oglesby) One of the alien Miradorn twin brothers who try to sell stolen goods to Quark. He vows revenge on Croden who kills his twin, Rok-Kel, during a robbery attempt. He is killed, while stalking Croden, in a Toh Maire explosion in the Chamra Vortex in the Gamma Quadrant. ("Vortex")

ALDARA
Cardassian Warship commanded by Gul Danar, which pursued Bajoran terrorist Tahna Los. ("Past Prologue")

ALLAM¡ARINE
Successful completion of a shap in the game of chula. Also part of Chandra's chant. ("Move Along Home")

ALPHA-CURRANT NECTAR
Juice beverage, priceless in the Wadi Culture. ("Move Along Home")

ALPHA QUADRANT
Section of space where DS9 is located and where the reputation of the Ferengi is bad and their profits are low. ("The Nagus")

ALTONIAN BRAIN TEASER
A multi-hued, spherical, floating puzzle which responds to neural-theta waves through concentration. The goal is to turn the sphere into a solid color. It requires focus and clarity of thought. ("A Man Alone")

ALTORAN TRADER
Unidentified person whom Ah-Kel says he purchased an egg-like ahb-jadah bauble from. ("Vortex")

ANARA
Female Bajoran assistant to O'Brien in Ops. ("The Forsaken")

ANDEVIAN TWO
Planet where the forth moon at dawn is supposedly spectacular. ("The Forsaken")

ANDORIAN SILK
A precious fabric imported from the planet Andor. Quark tries to tempt Odo with a suit made of this valuable fabric. ("Q-Less")

ANDORIANS
Blue-skinned, white-haired aliens with Antenna. An Andorian freighter arrived at DS9

carrying new, anti-grav tractors. (See Classic Trek episode "Journey To Babel" also DS9 episode "The Nagus")

ANDROS TWO-B

Bajor Eight's lower moon, where the rendezvous between Klingon sisters, Lursa and B'Etor, and Tahna Los was to occur. ("Past Prologue")

ANNULAR CONTAINMENT FIELD

Setting on a transporter. ("Dramatis Personae")

ANTI-GRAV TRACTORS

Part of the cargo of the Andorian freighter. ("The Nagus")

ANTI-LEPTON INTERFERENCE

Cardassian method to cut off DS9's subspace communications with Starfleet. ("Emissary")

ANTI-MATTER CONVERTER

When combined with Bilitrium, the anti-matter converter can make a powerful bomb. Tahna Los was attempting to use the two components for his terrorist activities. ("Past Prologue")

APHASIA

Disease that strikes the DS9 crew making them unable to communicate with one another. It was defined by Bashir as "a perceptual dysfunction in which the oral and visual stimuli are incorrectly processed by the brain." The incubation period varies with each individual. It is highly adaptable and airborne. Within 12 hours, the virus begins attacking the nervous system, creates a high fever, and would eventually cause death. Both Odo and Quark seem to be immune. ("Babel")

I'm constantly on guard against having Kira come across as a man.
--Nana Visitor

APHASIA DEVICE

Small electronic circuit made with a diboridium core power source, that, when accidentally triggered, caused aphasia throughout DS9. Originally planted 18 years previous by Bajoran terrorists, it was meant to target the Cardassians. ("Babel")

AQUINO, ENSIGN

Crewmember that was thought to have been killed in a power conduit when he was trying to fix it. Later it was discovered that his death was no accident, and that Neela was responsible because Aquino got too close to discovering her plan. ("In The Hands Of The Prophets")

ARBAZAN

Alien race in the Federation. Taxco is the ambassador who visits DS9, representing her people. They are supposedly a sexually repressed race. ("The Forsaken")

ARBITER

Bajoran legal judge like the one that presided over Dax's extradition hearing. Els Renora, a white haired female, handled Dax's case as Arbiter. ("Dax")

ARCHAEOLOGICAL COUNCIL

Branch of the Daystrom Institute from which Professor Woo once suspended Vash. ("Q-Less")

ARCHIVAL RECORDS

Bajoran record library. ("Babel")

ARCYBITE MINING REFINERIES

Located in the Clarius System, these were taken over by the Ferengi, Nava. ("The Nagus")

ARGINE

Explosive component of a Ferengi locator bomb. ("The Nagus")

ARGOSIAN

Alien Lieutenant who once threw a drink in Sisko's face. Sisko had to be restrained by Curzon. ("Dax")

ARGOSIAN SECTOR

Sector of space. ("Babel")

ARTIFACTS

Brought back from the Gamma Quadrant by Vash. They include a 30 odd centimeter tall, stone statue from the Verath System; an assortment of gems— eight kilograms; a gold necklace; a bronze & gold dagger—about 25 centimeters; and a glowing geode. ("Q-Less")

ARVA NODES

Device on Tosk's Gamma Quadrant ship that converts space matter into fuel. Similar to a Federation Ram Scoop. ("Captive Pursuit")

ASOTH

Alien in Quark's who forces Quark to eat bad Kohlanese stew that Quark served him. ("Babel")

ASSAY OFFICE

Storage and declaration facility where Vash inventories and stores her Gamma Quadrant artifacts. Supposedly the most secure area of DS9 since it is surrounded by individual force-fields. Vash stored her artifacts in cubicle 19. ("Q-Less")

ASSAY OFFICE CLERK (Van Epperson)

Bajoran who runs DS9's Assay office. ("Q-Less")

AUBERGINE STEW

Specialty of Benjamin Sisko's father, who was a gourmet chef. ("Emissary")

AZNA

Dish Dax orders in Quarks. Apparently she has been eating it for years and has tried many times to convince Sisko to eat it too. She claims that it would put

years on his life, but Sisko passes on it anyway. Azna is usually served steamed. ("A Man Alone")

B

BAJOR

Beautiful world that space-station Deep Space Nine orbits. It was occupied by Cardassians for 60 years, and stripped of its resources before being abandoned, leaving the Bajoran people without a means of being self-sustaining. Ruling parties on Bajor are at each other's throats, keeping them from being admitted into the Federation. Bajoran people are spiritual, under leadership of the Kai, they worship the Prophets.

With the discovery of the Wormhole, Bajor's importance to the Federation has dramati-

cally increased. ("Emissary")

Bajor Eight, in the same system, hosts a lower moon called Andros Two-B. ("Past Prologue")

Visitors often attend Bajor's biggest festival—the Gratitude Festival, where they view the spectacular Fire Caverns. ("The Nagus")

Bajor is the largest planet in its system and has three moons. ("The Nagus")

The Bajorans have no treaties with the Klaestrons, in fact are enemies because of the Klaestron alliance with the Cardassians. ("Dax")

DS9 is technically in Bajoran Space. ("Dax")

Bajor's North Eastern District is home to the Ilvian Medical complex. ("Babel")

Its people are still divided, such as the Paqu and the Navot, rival clans. And they need to be united. For that reason, stories like that of the Dal'Rok were

created. There is an old saying on Bajor: "The land and the people are one." ("The Storyteller")

Bajor's fifth moon is Jeraddo, the site of their first large scale energy transfer created by tapping the molten core. Tessipates are the unit of measurement of land on Bajor. ("Progress")

Bajor - One location on the planet is Gallitepp, site of a Cardassian forced labor camp. ("Duet")

BAJORAN DEATH CHANT

Kira recites the chant when Opaka dies. It goes like this:
Ahn Kay Ya, Coh Ma Ra
Ow Kay Ya, Ay Ya Vasy
("Battle Lines")

BAJOR EIGHT

Eighth planet in the Bajor system. Its lower moon, used in a rendezvous between the Klingon sisters Lursa and B'Etor and Tahna Los, is called Andros Two-B. Bajor Eight is home to six Bajoran colonies. ("Past Prologue")

BAJORAN PROVISIONAL GOVERNMENT

Gave Starfleet permission to establish Federation presence in the Bajor system following the occupation of Cardassian forces. ("Emissary")

B'KAAZI

Alien race of Jas-qal, Nog's assistant in his theft attempt. ("Emissary") (novelization)

BALOSNEE SIX

Vacation spot considered by Grand Nagus Zek. The soothing harmonies of the tides there can cause the most stimulating hallucinations. ("The Nagus")

BALTRIM

(Terrence Evans) Old male Bajoran living on Jeraddo who refused to leave. His companions, Mullibok and Keena also

refused to leave during the Bajoran evacuation. Baltrim, along with Keena, was rendered speechless by the Cardassians 18 years previous. Shortly after that, they escaped to Jeraddo. Because of the Cardassians, they fear people in uniform. They were removed forcibly. ("Progress")

BANERIAM HAWK

Type of bird Quark compares Odo to when he says he's just sitting there waiting for prey. ("If Wishes Were Horses")

BARBO

Ferengi cousin of Quark recently released from the Tarahong Detention Center, where he was held for selling defective warp drives with Quark. ("The Nagus")

BASEBALL

A game that Jake & Sisko play on the holodeck. Sisko used it as an example to explain linear existence to the inhabitants of the Wormhole. ("Emissary")

According to Nog, baseball is a stupid game that even humans stopped playing hundreds of years ago. ("The Storyteller")

Bokai says baseball died because people didn't have time for it anymore. It diminished in popularity in the mid-twenty-second century. In the '42 series, there were only 300 people in the stands. ("If Wishes Were Horses")

BASHIR, DR. JULIAN

(Siddig EL Fadil) Medical Officer, fresh out of Starfleet, assigned to DS9. At twenty-seven years old, Bashir is enthusiastic about his 'frontier' assignment, and enamored with science officer Dax. He had his choice of any job in the fleet and chose DS9. ("Emissary")

He was chosen by Garak to be an informer/liaison between the Cardassians and the Federation. ("Past Prologue")

He is remarkably poor at the Altonian Brain teaser even though he claims to love puzzles. He is persistent, energetic, and very excitable. ("A Man Alone")

He can be very full of himself when analyzing his medical skills. He was taken over by Vantika when the criminal stored his consciousness in Bashir. His authorization Code is 4121. ("The Passenger")

He will not hesitate to scream when frightened. ("Move Along Home")

Julian manages a date with Vash, much to the displeasure of Q, who cuts it short. He often resorts to bragging to win over the opposite sex. He was salutatorian in his Starfleet Medical class, claiming he was one question away from Valedictorian. ("Q-Less")

He gallantly tries to rescue Dax from kidnappers, but instead is knocked unconscious. ("Dax")

Bashir has skill in computers. He managed to repair the broken computer of the crashed Runabout. ("Battle Lines")

Bashir claims that O'Brien's opinion means a lot to him, and that he has a tendency to run off at the mouth. Bashir outranks O'Brien. ("The Storyteller")

With his quick-thinking, Bashir saves the life of three Federation Ambassadors from a DS9 corridor fire. ("The Forsaken")

He refuses to give up pursuing Dax even after spending time with a Betazoid Envoy and a Junior Lieutenant at a reception for Captain Stadius. ("If Wishes Were Horses")

While teaching at Rutgers, I sang with such jazz artists as Jon Henricks, Butch Morris, and Lester Bowie. For years I straddled the fence between the academic and the performance
—Avery Brooks

BELLOS SEVEN

A Cardassian prison where the Bajoran bio-engineer Dekon Elig was locked up before he was killed in an escape attempt on Stardate 39355. ("Babel")

BETAZED

Planet where Vash is not welcome. (("Q-Less")) Also home to Ambassador Lwaxana Troi (("The Forsaken")) and the envoy Dr. Bashir had a romantic interlude with. (Also see ("The Storyteller"):TNG) ("If Wishes Were Horses")

BETAZOID

Humanoid Federation race that has telepathic and empathic powers, although those powers don't extend to reading Dopterians and Ferengi. The Betazed Ambassador is Lwaxana Troi, mother of the half-Betazoid ship's Counselor Deanna Troi of the U.S.S. Enterprise. ("The Forsaken")

BETAZOID ENVOY

Woman from Betazed with whom Dr. Bashir had a romantic interlude with. ("If Wishes Were Horses")

B'ETOR

Klingon woman of the House of Duras. Sister of Lursa. Arrived on DS9 after trying to gain power of the Klingon High Council which resulted in a brief civil war. Until their DS9 arrival, the renegade sisters were in hiding. They came to DS9 to get payment from Tahna Los. (Also see ST:TNG episode "Redemption" and DS9 episode "Past Prologue")

BILITRIUM

A rare crystalline element that can be an incredibly powerful source of energy when used in conjunction with an anti-matter converter. The Klingon sisters Lursa and B'Etor were supposed to deliver a cylinder of bilitrium to

Tahna Los in a shady deal, in which he planned to destroy the Wormhole. ("Past Prologue")

BIPOLAR TORCH

Cutting tool, stronger than phasers. It can cut through a Toranium bulk-head. ("The Forsaken")

BIRD OF PREY

Type of Klingon ship. ("Dramatis Personae")

BIO-REGENERATIVE FIELD

Liquid-filled container used in regenerating biological material. Can be used in the cloning process. ("A Man Alone")

BOKAI, HARMON "BUCK"

(Keone Young) Legendary baseball player considered to be the greatest baseball hitter of all- time. Jake plays with his image in the holosuites. (("The Storyteller")) Even though he has been dead for 200 years, Bokai followed Jake home from the holo-suite. A personal hero to Ben Sisko, he explained to the commander how much his caring meant to him. It turned out that this version was an alien trying to study human imagination.

Bokai played as #49 with the London Kings. He hit the homer that won the '42 series in the 22nd century and broke Joe DiMaggio's consecutive streak. He was a switch-hitter that played third base. He hit over 20 home runs from the right side in each of his first three years in the majors. Sisko says he was the best that ever played. ("If Wishes Were Horses")

BOLIANS

Pale-blue skinned aliens. Serving in Starfleet. Hranok, tactical officer aboard the Saratoga is one. ("Emissary") (novelization) Also the race of a woman Quark caught cheating and kicked out of his casino. ("Captive Pursuit")

The Federation ambassador Vadosia is also a Bolian. ("The Forsaken") (Also see ST:TNG episode "Allegiance")

BORG

Formidable adversary of the Federation. Half organic, half robotic. Responsible for the massacre at Wolf 359 where the U.S.S. Saratoga, Ben Sisko's ship was destroyed, and Sisko's wife, Jennifer, was killed. ("Emissary")

BORG SHIP

Huge cube of spaceborne metal layered with randomly placed conduits, piping, etc. It has regenerative qualities. Nearly unbeatable with superior offensive capabilities. The interior harbors honeycombed compartments for individual Borg's recharging. The ship actually reflects the Borg's hive mentality. ("Emissary")

BOYER, ENSIGN

Crewperson under O'Brien who can pilot a runabout as well as he can. O'Brien tries to get the Ensign to escort Bashir to Bajor, so he wouldn't have to. ("The Storyteller")

BRAX

Planet where Q is known as the God of Lies. ("Q-Less")

BROOCH

Lwaxana Troi's hair brooch made of latinum. It is priceless and has been in her family for 36 generations. It was stolen by a Dopterian in Quark's bar. ("The Forsaken")

BROIK

Ferengi assistant to Quark, caught cheating on the Dabo table by the Wadi. ("Move Along Home")

I like being other people. I'm really an actor all the time. Before being discovered in the part I was always a comedian and was also involved in drama. I feel everyday living is acting. So I've really enjoyed it so far because it's still me, but I'm being recognized now
—Cirroc Lofton

BUTCHER OF GAL-LITEPP

Informal title given to Gul Darhe'el, leader of the Bajoran labor camp Gallitepp. ("Duet")

C

CABRODINE

An explosive used to blow up the school on DS9. It is common and easily obtained. ("In The Hands Of The Prophets")

CARDASSIA

Home planet of the Cardassians. ("Duet")

CARDASSIANS:

Race from Cardassia, reptilian-like with ridged-forehead. At one time they occupied Bajor. They also built the DS9 space station. Before they left, they decided to have some 'fun' and vandalized DS9, killing 4 Bajorans who were trying to protect their shops. They had been oppressing the Bajoran people for 60 years. They stripped the planet of every resource before abandoning Bajor, leaving the Bajorans without a means of being self-sustaining. Cardassians are famous for treating their prisoners badly, ("Emissary") including using torture methods designed to keep their prisoners alive. ("Past Prologue")

Long-time allies of the Klaestrons. ("Dax")

They left behind a piece of circuitry attached to the replicators that causes the aphasia disease. ("Babel")

During their occupation of Bajor, the Cardassians altered the river Glyrhond for mining purposes, upsetting the boundary for rival Bajoran clans. Cardassians were responsible for the killing of Paqu Tetrarch, Varis Sul's Bajoran parents. ("The Storyteller")

During their oppression of Bajor, they would often render Bajorans speechless. People like Baltrim and Keena were muted before their escape to Jeraddo. Mullibok had to spend time in one of their work camps. It is said that Cardassians pay their bills. ("Progress")

They ran a forced labor camp at Gallitepp on Bajor. It was led by Gul Darhe'el and was the site of the worst atrocities against the Bajorans. ("Duet")

CARDASSIAN GUARD

Military division broken into orders, for example, the Seventh Order. Usually the Cardassians have three ships to an order. ("Emissary")

CARGO BAY FOUR

Bay where Odo rounds up the mutinous crewmembers to administer the interference program. ("Dramatis Personae")

CARGO DRONE

Type of crewless ship O'Brien occasionally wishes he were transferred to. "No people, No complaints," he says. ("Babel")

CELESTIAL TEMPLE

Legendary home of the Prophets—the Bajoran gods. Also the place where the 9 orbs called Tears of the Prophets originated. Later the Celestial Temple was considered to be the Wormhole near Bajor. ("Emissary")

CHAMRA VORTEX

Colorful section of space in the Gamma Quadrant where Croden claimed the colony of Changelings existed, tucked away in an asteroid belt. Pockets of explosive gases called Toh Maire make navigating in the Vortex dangerous. ("Vortex")

CHANDRA

(Clara Bryant) Small girl in the Wadi game of

chula who plays a child's game similar to hop-scotch. Players must repeat her actions to pass the force-field. ("Move Along Home")

CHANGELING

Another name for Shapeshifter given to Odo's species by Croden from the Gamma Quadrant. Supposedly Changelings set up a colony in the Chamra Vortex, but that claim was proven false. The only proof they exist, other than Odo, is a shapeshifting stone. ("Vortex")

CHILDREN

Aboard DS9, besides Jake and Nog, there are 12 other children, ranging in age from 8 to 16. That doesn't include two year-old Molly O'Brien. ("A Man Alone")

CHLOROBICROBES

Farming chemicals sprayed on Katterpod beans to improve their quality. ("Progress")

CHULA

A strategy game brought to DS9 by the Wadi. It is played on an elaborate, maze-like, six leveled board with four onyx figurines. In reality, when Quark plays, the players are living, namely, Kira, Dax, Sisko, & Bashir. The object is to 'move along home.' ("Move Along Home")

CLARIUS SYSTEM

Home star system to the Arcybite Mining Refineries which were taken over by the Ferengi, Nava. ("The Nagus")

CLONE

A replicated person developed from cells or DNA of the donor. Even though the DNA is identical, certain cloning methods cause a gene-sequence degradation, making it possible to tell the copy from the original. ("A Man Alone")

COBB, TY

(Kevin McDermott) Baseball player recreated in Sisko's mind when communicating with the inhabitants of the wormhole. ("Emissary") (novelization)

COLADRIUM FLOW

Part of Tosk's ship that was damaged. O'Brien has no clue to what it is or how to fix it. ("Captive Pursuit")

COMBADGE

Communications insignia carried by all station personnel. O'Brien deliberately removed his to avoid being located. ("Captive Pursuit")

CONSTABLE

Title given to Odo. ("Emissary")

CORADO ONE

Nearby colony to DS9. It has a transmitter array that DS9 can link into. ("The Forsaken")

COROPHIZINE

Medicine used to counter a secondary infection in aphasia patients. Used in dosage of 30 cc's. ("Babel")

CORUNDIUM

Mineral alloy used in building the 'Pup" probe. ("The Forsaken")

CRODEN

(Cliff DeYoung) Alien brought back by the Klingons from the Gamma Quadrant. He kills Rok-Kel while committing a robbery set up by Quark. Croden is from Rakhar where he is wanted for the murder of two security guards, who he claims killed his two wives. He tricks Odo into taking him to an asteroid to find his daughter, Yareth, by telling him of the existence of other Changelings. After saving Odo's life, Odo allows Croden and Yareth to escape on a Vulcan ship. ("Vortex")

CROSS

A roll in the game of Dabo ("If Wishes Were Horses") & ("The Forsaken")

CROW

Manager of the 22nd century baseball team, the London Kings. He moved Buck Bokai to second in the batting order. ("If Wishes Were Horses")

CROWN OF THE FIRST MOTHER

Object Vash stole from the Planet Myrmidon. ("Q-Less")

CRYO-STASIS

Medical procedure used to treat the severely wounded. It probably it slows down body functions for easier repair. ("Dramatis Personae")

CUBICLE 19

Where Vash stored her artifacts in DS9's Assay office. ("Q-Less")

D

DABO

Gambling game played in Quark's casino. ("Emissary")

Similar to roulette in that a wheel is spun, but it differs in that it uses pins and crosses in its outcome. ("Move Along Home")

In Dabo, one cross or two crosses are bad Dabo rolls. ("If Wishes Were Horses")

DABO GIRL

(Diana Cignoni) Hostess of the gambling game Dabo in Quark's casino. ("Emissary") & ("A Man Alone")

One red-headed alien named Miss Sarda was tricked by Quark into signing an agreement that say she owes him sexual favors. It was an agreement on page 21, subsection D, paragraph 12 of her employment contract. ("Captive Pursuit")

[O'Brien] was developed over a long period, about four years, and that really helps an actor.
—Colm Meany

DAIMON

Ferengi leadership title for ship commanders. Lwaxana refers to the one that had a crush on her before he kidnapped her and her daughter. ("The Forsaken")

DAL'ROK

A terrible cloud creature with that produces wind and lightening. It lives in the Bajoran woods and descends for five nights every year at the end of the harvest. Only the Sirah can defeat it by telling a loud ritual tale. But the Dal'Rok doesn't register on any sensor scans because, in reality, it is the fear of the villagers taken on physical form to unite the villagers. It is accomplished through a fragment of the Tear of the Prophet orb. ("The Storyteller")

DAUGHTER OF THE FIFTH HOUSE

Part of Lwaxana Troi's title. It reflects her Betazed nobility. ("The Forsaken")

DAYSTROM INSTITUTE

Scientific facility on Earth, which is very interested in Vash's exploration of the Gamma Quadrant. Professor Woo, who is a member, once suspended Vash's membership from the archaeological council. The name of the institute was probably taken from Dr. Daystrom, creator of M-5. (See Classic Trek episode "The Ultimate Computer" and the DS9 episode "Q-Less")

DAX DUPLICATE

An overly affectionate replica of Jadzia Dax who does her best to seduce Dr. Bashir and fulfill his wishes. It turned out that she was an advanced alien lifeform, trying to study human imagination. ("If Wishes Were Horses")

DAX

Symbiotic part of Jadzia Dax. The worm-like slug inside her is well over 300 years old and has been hosted by five other bodies, including the late Curzon Dax. Together with the host, all memories and personalities are maintained. ("A Man Alone")

She has been a mother three times and a father, twice and claims she wasn't good at being either. ("The Nagus")

Dax was wanted for treason and the murder of General Ardelon Tandro, 30 years previous to DS9, when the host was Curzon. He served as the Federation mediator during the Klaestron civil war. Dax transferred from Curzon to Jadzia, two years previous to her being stationed on DS9, and had been friends with Sisko for 18-20 years. ("Dax")

Dax hasn't been a female for over 80 years.

She had forgotten how much attention she receives. ("Babel")

DAX, CURZON

(Frank Owen Smith) Previous humanoid host to the Trill symbiote, Dax. He was an old man when the transfer was made, and was also a close friend of Ben Sisko. ("Emissary") He was a mentor, and a second father to him. In fact, they would attend the Rujian Steeplechase together and once double-dated with seven foot Ruji sisters that Curzon knew. He supposedly loved the races. Curzon was Dax's fifth host. He used to beat Sisko regularly at bare-fisted Juro-counter-punch. ("A Man Alone")

While serving as Federation mediator, during the civil war on Klaestron Four, he supposedly murdered General Ardelon Tandro. The death occurred 30 years previous to Dax serving aboard DS9. He

> *I find it incredibly irresponsible and ultimately ludicrous to suggest that television is somehow responsible for problems that we've faced for decades, for centuries*
> — Avery Brooks

was later cleared of charges. Tandro and Curzon were best of friends before his death. Curzon died two years previous to Dax being stationed on DS9. According to Sisko, Curzon tended to be cavalier about his life and responsibilities and had more flaws than the average Trill; Curzon drank too much, and was a little too interested in woman. A statement proven by the fact that he had an affair with his best friends, Tandro's, wife Enina Tandro. It is her confession of that fact that cleared him of murder. Sisko and Curzon had been friends for 16-18 years prior to his death. He taught Ensign Sisko about art, science, and diplomacy. ("Dax")

Curzon always warned Sisko about his temper, and even had to deck him to prevent him from killing an Argosian Lieutenant who threw a drink in his face. ("Dax")

He supposedly took perverse pleasure in assigning Ben Sisko to take care of VIP quests. ("The Forsaken")

DAX, JADZIA LIEUTENANT (Terry Farrell)

Trill Science Officer assigned to DS9. Her host body Jadzia is twenty- eight, but the worm-like slug symbiote inside her, Dax, is well over three-hundred. Previously, Dax, when in the host body of Curzon, a male, was close friends with Benjamin Sisko. Sisko still calls her 'old man' from time to time. She is constantly fending off propositions from love-struck Dr. Bashir. ("Emissary")

She was decorated on her very first mission by a Vulcan admiral. ("Dramatis Personae")

She has over 300 years of scientific experience. ("The Forsaken") When younger, she was a champion window breaker. ("Duet")

Her remarkable powers of concentration enable her to nearly master an Altonian Brain Teaser which she has been practicing at for over 140 years. Jadzia is the sixth host for the trill symbiote Dax. ("A Man Alone")

Jadzia had already been host to Dax for two years before being assigned to DS9. She is charged with the murder, 30 years previous, of General Ardelon Tandro, when Curzon Dax was host, and was Federation mediator on Tandro's planet Klaestron Four. She decides to remain loyal and quiet about the accusation to protect Enina Tandro, with whom Curzon Dax had an affair. Before becoming a host, at age 26, she earned premier academic degrees in exobiology, zoology, astrophysics, and exoarchaeology. ("Dax")

Dax once turned down a date with Morn even though she feels his wiry hairs make him look cute. ("Progress")

She once helped the Federation deliver rain-inducing technology to Kelton Four. ("Dramatis Personae")

DEEP SPACE NINE

Space-station surrounding Bajor. On Stardate 46388.2, Commander Benjamin Sisko took over as commander in a joint effort between the Federation and the Bajoran Provisional government. Upon arriving, they found that the Cardassian-built space-station was stripped, vandalized and left virtually defenseless. It is described as one of the most remote outposts in the galaxy. The station is powered by six working thrusters, and has great difficulty being moved, although it can be done. DS9 has limited shields and limited defense capabilities, namely six photon torpedoes fired

to warn the Cardassians. The docking ring is a very vulnerable part of the station. With the discovery of the Wormhole, the station's importance has dramatically increased. ("Emissary")

It is located in the Alpha Quadrant (("The Nagus")) and is technically in Bajoran space and thereby governed by Bajoran extradition processes. ("Dax")

It was built 18 years previous to Federation coming on board, it is referred to as the Old Cardassian mining station by Bajorans. ("Babel")

Three hundred people reside on the station. Its primary purpose is to monitor the wormhole. On the average, five or six ships dock there a week. The station is divided into 19 sections, and has a Habitat Ring with guest quarters located in corridor H-12-A. ("The Forsaken")

It is equipped with shields and much of it is made from the Cardassian metal Duranium. ("Captive Pursuit")

DEFENSE NET
A security arrangement of satellites surrounding the Penal Colony Moon in the Gamma Quadrant. ("Battle Lines")

DELANEY, ENSIGN
(Lily Mariye) Young, female Ops officer on the U.S.S. Saratoga. Killed in Borg massacre at Wolf 359. ("Emissary") (novelization)

DELTA QUADRANT
Another Quadrant of space Q wants to explore with Vash. ("Q-Less")

DEKON ELIG
Bajoran geneticist and bio-engineer who created the Aphasia device, he was last seen in a Cardassian prison camp, Bellos Seven,

nine years previous. He was killed during an escape attempt on Stardate 39355. He was a former member of the Higa Metar sect of the Bajoran Underground. ("Babel")

DENORIOS ASTEROID BELT

A charged plasma field in space, near Bajor which all ships try to avoid. However, in the 22nd century, Kai Taluno's ship was disabled in the belt and he had a vision where the heavens opened up and nearly swallowed his ship. At least five of the orbs or Tears of the Prophets were found here. Also the site of unusually severe neutrino disturbances. Also the place where Odo was found. ("Emissary")

DERMATIRAELIAN PLASTISCINE

Medicine taken to maintain skin resilience following cosmetic alteration. Marritza was tak-

ing large doses to maintain his appearance of Gul Darhe'el. ("Duet")

DEURIDIUM

Scarce substance needed by the Kobliad race to stabilize their cell structure and prolong their life. Can be found in the Gamma Quadrant. It would cause evacuation of a system if released into space. ("The Passenger")

DIBORIDIUM

Element used in the core power source of the device found that caused the aphasia aboard DS9. It is an element used greatly in Cardassian technology. The device was installed 18 years previous. ("Babel")

DIFFERENTIAL MAG-NETOMER

Invention by O'Brien to scan planets to search for specific metals in the missing Runabout's hull. ("Battle Lines")

DiMAGGIO, JOE

Twentieth Century baseball great. Buck Bokai went on the break his consecutive streak. ("If Wishes Were Horses")

DOCKING RINGS

Sections of Space Station DS9 where ships can dock. It is very vulnerable to heavy damage during an attack. One of the rings is called the Forward Docking Ring.

DOLAMIDE

Valuable component in Cardassian weapons manufacturing. The Valerians sold dolamide to the Cardassians during their occupation of Bajor. Dolamide is also used for reactors, power generators, and short range transports. ("Dramatis Personae")

DOLBARGY SLEEPING TRANCE

Hypnotic state taught by Maihar'du to Zek which enabled him to fake death. ("The Nagus")

DOPTERIAN

Alien race related to the Ferengi. They have brown skin, ridged noses, bumpy heads with one ring around the back half. One is caught stealing Lwaxana Troi's broach in Quark's. ("The Forsaken") DORAN

Jennifer Sisko's closest friend and next door neighbor aboard the Saratoga. (Lynnda Ferguson) ("Emissary")

DROLOCK

The Prime Asemety of the Verath System in the Gamma Quadrant during the 19th Dynasty. A statue of him was found by Vash. ("Q-Less")

DS9

Guest quarters are located in Corridor H-12-A. ("The Forsaken") (Also see listing DEEP SPACE NINE)

DURANIUM

Metal used in Cardassian construction. It is nearly impossible for a scanning device to penetrate it. DS9's conduits are made from it. ("Captive Pursuit")

DURANIUM ALLOY

Metal used in SHIP building. Dax and O'Brien found remains of it from the destroyed hull of a Klingon ship. It emits a magnetic field that can mask sensors ("Dramatis Personae")

DURANIUM SHADOWS

Illusion used to fool the Cardassians into thinking DS9 has greater weapon-power than it has. ("Emissary")

DURAS

Klingon "House" or family which tried to take power of the Klingon High Council. Sisters Lursa and B'Etor paid a visit to DS9. (Also see ST:TNG episode "Redemption") ("Past Prologue")

DURG

Alien mercenary Quark hired to help Vantika hijack the deuridium shipment. Quark apparently had something to do with his release from a Cardassian prison. ("The Passenger")

E

E-J-SEVEN INTERLOCK

Tool O'Brien misplaced. Later it was found with a murdered crewman, Ensign Aquino. It is used to close security seals and could be used to access every critical system on the station. It is made out of tritanium. ("In The Hands Of The Prophets")

ELANU FOUR

Planet where Dax and Sisko were involved in a wild goose chase. ("Dramatis Personae")

Visitor readily admits that Major Kira is a revamped version of Ensign Ro Laren from THE NEXT GENERATION.

ELS RENORA

(Anne Haney) One hundred year old, white-haired female Bajoran Arbiter who presides over Dax's extradition hearing. She has a great-granddaughter about the same age as Jadzia Dax. ("Dax")

EMBRYONIC LIFE-FORM

Winged energy being shaped like a manta ray, which disrupted the energy patterns of the station until it exploded in space from its egg-like form and headed back to the Gamma Quadrant where it was originally found by Vash. ("Q-Less")

EMISSARY

Bajoran title for Sisko, because he made contact with the Prophets or wormhole inhabitants. ("Emissary")

EMULATOR MODULE

Part of DS9's computer system. ("The Forsaken")

ENERGY DISTRIBUTION NET

On Cardassian ships it is somehow involved with the computer system. Odo sabotaged this system to create a diversion for Sisko and Dax, enabling them to discover the Wormhole. ("Emissary")

ENERGY MATRIX

Cause of the mutinies aboard the Klingon ship Toh'Kaht and DS9. It was released from the energy spheres into the individual's brains. ("Dramatis Personae")

ENERGY SPHERES

Discovered by the Klingons in the Gamma Quadrant on the Fifth planet of an unnamed system. Once they opened the telepathic archives of the ancient race, the Klingon crew began having mutiny problems which they brought to DS9. Previously the power of the spheres destroyed

the Saltah'na race. It infected all with an energy matrix. ("Dramatis Personae")

ENNIS

Humanoid people at war on a penal colony in the Gamma Quadrant. Enemy of the Nol-Ennis. Golin Shel-la is their leader. They can never die, thanks to a bio-mechanical presence, and they can never leave the colony, even though they have been there for an eternity. ("Battle Lines")

ENTERPRISE, U.S.S.

Starship captained by Jean-Luc Picard who's body was taken over by the Borg and renamed Locutus. ("Emissary")

EPSILON HYDRA SEVEN

Planet where the Royal Museum is located. Vash is banned from there. ("Q-Less")

ERABUS PRIME

Planet where Vash was bitten by a deadly insect, which Q saved her from. ("Q-Less")

ERRIKANG SEVEN

Planet where Q almost got Vash killed. ("Q-Less")

EXARCH

Title given to the Leader of the Nehelik province on the Planet Rahkar in the Gamma Quadrant. ("Vortex")

F

FALOW

(Joel Brooks) Leader of the Wadi race who visit DS9 from the Gamma Quadrant. He is the Master Surchid of the Wadi. ("Move Along Home")

FAREN KAG

(Jim Jansen) Magistrate of the Bajoran village where the Sirah protects the people from the Dal'Rok ("The Storyteller")

FAHLEENA THREE

Planet visited by the Valerian ship Sherval Das. It is one of the stops the Valerians use to secure dolamide. ("Dramatis Personae")

FERENGI

Big-eared, sharp toothed alien race who are motivated by profit and greed. Quark, Nog, and Rom are Ferengi. Education for the Ferengi is based on a work study approach, basically the student is thrown into the cut-throat competition of the Ferengi commerce. Ferengi do not respect females, ("A Man Alone") and they can't have their mind read by telepathic Betazoids, nor can their cousin

race, the Dopterians. ("The Forsaken")

FIFTEEN DELTA

Quadrant on Bajor's moon, Jeraddo, where Mullibok lived. ("Progress")

FIRE-CAVERNS

Scenic spot on Bajor that Jake would like to visit. ("The Nagus")

FIRST CONTACT PROCEDURES

Guidelines Starfleet crewmembers must follow when encountering a new race for the first time. Dax recommends postponing formal procedures in their first contact with Tosk of the Gamma Quadrant. ("Captive Pursuit")

FIRST RULE OF ACQUISITION

"Once you have their money, you never give it back." A Ferengi oath, part of a greater set of Rules. ("The Nagus")

He's [Sisko] not afraid to speak about how he feels. He's a deep thinker but, yet, a quick one. He makes decisions very quickly. He also has a great sense of humor. He's curious about everything.
—Avery Brooks

4100 RLX

Security Code used to protect subroutine A-N-A by Neela in her plot to kill Bareil. ("In The Hands Of The Prophets")

FOURTH ORDER

Nearby Cardassian reinforcements to Gul Jasad's Seventh order of the Cardassian Guard. ("Emissary")

FRUNALIAN SCIENCE VESSELS

Three of these ships requested to dock shortly after the discovery of the wormhole. ("Emissary")

G

GAGE, U.S.S.

One of the ships destroyed at the battle with the Borg at Wolf 359. ("Emissary")

GALIS

Female Bajoran friend of Kira's. She talks to her via video link. ("Babel")

GALLITEPP

Cardassian controlled forced labor camp on Bajor. As a result of a mining accident there, the survivors contracted Kalla-Nohra syndrome. Those survivors had always been a symbol to Bajorans of strength and courage. It was the site of the worst atrocities by the Cardassians. Kira, as part of the resistance, helped liberate the camp. ("Duet")

GAMMA QUADRANT

Section of space, unexplored by the Federation, 70 thousand light-years from Bajor. The Wormhole near Bajor empties into it less than 5 light-years from the Idran system. Little is known about it, except for information provided by the 22nd Quadros-One Probe. ("Emissary")

Being 70 thousand light years from Bajor on

the other side of the galaxy, the fastest Starship would take 67 years to reach it. ("Battle Lines")

Also a source of deuridium, ("The Passenger") and home to the Wadi Race, ("Move Along Home") and Croden, of the planet Rakhar, where he says Changelings, like Odo, originated, but he was misleading in that claim. The Chamra Vortex, where the Changeling colony supposedly existed is located here, and is peppered with pockets of exploding gas called Toh Maire. ("Vortex")

Vash has been exploring the quadrant for the past two years with the help of Q. She brought back many artifacts, including a pulsing geode that reeks havoc on DS9's energy fields. It is found out to be some kind of egg for a winged energy being from the Gamma Quadrant. Some cul-

tures in the Gamma Quadrant have histories dating back millions of years. ("Q-Less")

Home to the Nol-Ennis and the Ennis, two groups at war on a penal colony on a moon surrounded by satellites. The moon is in a binary Star System. ("Battle Lines")

Home of Tosk, the reptilian being that arrived through the wormhole being chased in a game of life and death. He was the first visitor to DS9 from the Gamma Quadrant. ("Captive Pursuit")

The 'Pup' probe originated in the Gamma Quadrant, ("The Forsaken") as well as the energy spheres that caused the mutiny problems aboard the Klingon vessel and DS9. The spheres once destroyed a Gamma Quadrant race called the Saltah'na. ("Dramatis Personae")

GAMZIAN WINE

A beverage served at Quark's ("Q-Less")/("The Storyteller")

GANGES

One of the three Runabouts stationed at DS9. It returned to the station drained of power with Dax, Ensign Pauley, and Vash on board. The doors needed to be pried open manually. Later, it was discovered that one of the artifacts Vash was carrying had caused the power drain. ("Q-Less")

It was also used by Sisko and O'Brien in tracking Tahna Los, ("Past Prologue") and used by Odo to return Croden to Rahkar. ("Vortex")

Dax and Kira also checked out the moon Jeraddo for evacuation stragglers from the Ganges Runabout. ("Progress")

GARAK

(Andrew Robinson) Cardassian who remained on the DS9 station, reportedly to be the eyes and ears for his fellow Cardassians. He owns a clothing shop on the Promenade. He is involved with shady dealings, notably with the Klingon sisters, Lursa and B'Etor, but yet allows Dr. Bashir to 'discover' his plans. ("Past Prologue")

GARANIAN BOLITES

Small creatures used by Jake and Nog for mischievous purposes. When they crawl on a humanoid, they bring about a tremendous itching problem and cause the person to turn various colors. ("A Man Alone")

GARCIA

(Steven Davies) Bridge crew member killed in Borg massacre at Wolf 259. ("Emissary") (novelization)

GEODE

(Unofficial name) An iridescent gemstone

brought back from the Gamma Quadrant that caused havoc on DS9 when its graviton pulses interfere with the power grids. Q bids one million bars of gold-pressed latinum for the stone, shortly before the DS9 crew beams it off the station where it explodes in space, releasing a magnificent embryonic winged energy being resembling a manta ray, which soars back to the Gamma Quadrant through the wormhole. Its molecular density and refraction index is much higher than Promethean Quartz, which it was mistaken for. ("Q-Less")

GEORGE'S PARTY
Where Jennifer thought she had met Benjamin Sisko previously. ("Emissary")

GILGO BEACH
(Script spelling: GOGIL BEACH) Beach where Jennifer and Benjamin Sisko met. ("Emissary")

GLIAL CELL
Cells along the central nervous system that Vantika used to send a bio-coded message through, enabling him to impart his own consciousness into his host ("The Passenger")

GLYRHOND
Bajoran river that is the border between the Paqu and the Navot clans. A dispute was created when the Cardassians altered the flow of the river for mining purposes. It now flows 20 kilometers west of its former position. ("The Storyteller")

GLESSENE SECTOR
Sector of space. ("Babel")

GOLD-PRESSED LATINUM
Highly sought after unit of currency, traded in the form of bars. ("Past Prologue")

Remains of the Nagus run for twenty-bars ("The Nagus")

An egg-like bauble called an ahb-jadah was to be sold to Quark for 1000 bars. ("Vortex")

Q bids one million bars for the iridescent geode from the Gamma Quadrant. Vash will only accept it as currency, and bet Quark 5 bars that Q would beat Sisko in the fight. A statue from the Gamma Quadrant was sold for 36 bars, a dagger for 105 bars, and a necklace for 151 bars. ("Q-Less")

Four or five bars could buy 5 thousand wrappages of Yamok sauce, and 5 bars buys seven tessipates of Bajoran land. ("Progress")

GUNJI JACKDAW

An ostrich-like bird that appeared on the Promenade due to someone's imagination. ("If Wishes Were Horses")

GRAL

Ferengi who introduces himself as Quark's new best friend when Quark becomes Grand Nagus. Gral offers to protect him, subtly threatening him. ("The Nagus")

GRAND NAGUS ZEK

(Wallace Shawn) Very old leader of the Ferengi, he loves spending time in the holo-suites. He comes to DS9 to host a Ferengi economic summit, and to step down from his position as Nagus, because he says, "I'm just not as greedy as I used to be." A surprise to everyone, especially his son Krax, Quark is named his successor. He soon fakes death, through a sleeping trance, to test his son. He claims he hasn't had a vacation in eighty-five years. ("The Nagus")

I love the shows where Rosalind is involved and we get to play family situations. — Colm Meany

GRATITUDE FESTIVAL

The biggest Bajoran festival of the year. ("The Nagus")

GUEST QUARTERS

Cabins reserved for visiting dignitaries on DS9. They are located on H-12-A. ("The Forsaken")

GUL

Cardassian title for the ranking officer. ("Emissary")

GUL DANAR

Cardassian commander of the warship Aldara who pursued Bajoran criminal Tahna Los. ("Past Prologue")

GUL DARHE'EL

Cardassian leader of the Cardassian controlled forced labor camp Gallitepp, on Bajor. He is also called the Butcher of Gallitepp. He never contracted Kalla- Nohra Syndrome since he was away at the time of the mining accident—he was back on Cardassia being awarded the Proficient Service Medallion. But he did die in his sleep due to a massive cerebral hemorrhage, six years previous to Marritza's impersonation of him. He is buried under one of the largest military monuments on Cardassia. ("Duet")

GUL DUKAT

Former Cardassian Prefect of DS9, now Commander. He used to have Commander Sisko's office. ("Emissary") He negotiated for the release of Marritza. He later tells Sisko that Gul Darhe'el is dead. When he was on board DS9 he played Kalevian Montar with Odo at least once, and supposedly he cheated. ("Duet")

GUL JASAD

(Joel Swetow) Cardassian Commander of the reinforcement warships sent to locate Gul Dukat. He is of the Cardassian Guard,

Seventh order, and threatened then demanded the surrender of the space-station. ("Emissary")

H

H-12-A

Corridor on DS9 which houses the Guest Quarters. A plasma explosion injured three Ambassadors & Dr. Bashir there. ("The Forsaken")

HABITAT RING

Section of DS9 where day to day living activities take place. Also where the weapons are stored in Level 5, Section Three. ("Captive Pursuit")

HADRAN

Exarch of Nehelik province on the planet Rahkar in the Gamma Quadrant. It was Hadran that insisted on the

extradition of Croden. ("Vortex")

HANOLI SYSTEM

Star-system destroyed in the mid 23rd Century when a subspace rupture expanded over it. ("If Wishes Were Horses")

HANSON, ADMIRAL

Starfleet admiral who deployed ships to do battle at WOLF 359 with the BORG. ("Emissary") (novelization)

HOEK FOUR

Planet in the Lantar Nebula which is home to the Sampalo Relic. It is a place Q wishes to take Vash. ("Q-Less")

HARU OUTPOST

Kira still has nightmares about her raids there during her tenure in the Bajoran underground. She is not proud of her involvement. ("Past Prologue")

The Ferengi have become more and more comical, although they're not monkey-like any more. —Armin Shimmerman

HIGA METAR SECT

Terrorist branch of the Bajoran underground. Dekon Elig, geneticist developer of the aphasia device, was once a member. ("Babel")

HOEX

Ferengi rival of Turot ever since he bought out Turot's interest in the cargo port on Volchok Prime. ("The Nagus")

HOLODECK

Recreation area which projects a fantasy setting. It is where Ben Sisko talks to son Jake, trying to re-assure him about going to DS9. Setting is a covered bridge over a pond. Sisko offers to take the pond with them. ("Emissary")

HOLOSUITES

Individual mini-holodecks in Quark's, usually used for sexual holographic fantasies. However Dax uses one to practice concentra-tion with an Altonian Brain Teaser. ("A Man Alone") Jake Sisko uses them everyday to play baseball usually with Buck Bokai. ("If Wishes Were Horses")

A favorite recreation tool of the Grand Nagus. ("The Nagus")

HOLOSUITE ONE

Holosuite One is where Quark set up a phony business deal where a Miradorn, Rok-Kel, was killed by Croden in a robbery attempt. ("Vortex")

HOLOSUITE FOUR

Suite used by Ibudan's clone for a massage, and where he was killed by Ibudan. ("A Man Alone")

HOLOSUITE SIX

The Klingons wrecked the walls in Holosuite Six. ("Dramatis Personae")

HOLY RINGS OF BETAZED

A mark of nobility, Lwaxana Troi is heir to

the Rings. ("The Forsaken")

HON-TIHL

(Tom Towles) Klingon first officer of the Toh'Kaht. He was the only survivor when the ship emerged from the Wormhole. He died shortly thereafter. ("Dramatis Personae")

HOVATH

(Lawrence Monoson) Bajoran apprentice for nine years, and rightful successor to the position of Sirah. He attempts to kill O'Brien and regain his status. He knows the secret behind the Dal'Rok, and rescues O'Brien's failed attempt, proving himself to be the true Sirah. ("The Storyteller")

HRANOK, LIEUTENANT

Bolian tactical officer aboard the Saratoga. With his muscular form and greater strength, Hranok pulled Ben Sisko and Jake away from his wife's dead body and to

a rescue pod. ("Emissary") (novelization)

HUNT

A game in the Gamma Quadrant involving a Tosk, a reptilian intelligent being, bred exclusively to be hunted for sport. The punishment for the dishonor of the Tosk being captured alive, is living out his life in humiliation on public display. ("Captive Pursuit")

HUPYRIAN

Race of the Nagus servant, Maihar'du. Hupyrians are tall, have wrinkled faces and purplish hair, and can induce a death-like sleeping trance. Hupyrian servants are renowned for their devotion to their employers. ("The Nagus")

I

IBUDAN

A Bajoran who pops into Quark's casino and is immediately confronted by Odo who wants him off the station. He was a black-marketeer during the days of the Cardassian occupation, but a hero to some on Bajor. Odo once witnessed the death of a girl from whom Ibudan denied life-saving drugs because she couldn't pay. Odo sent him to Kran Tobal prison for murdering a Cardassian officer, but the provisional government set him free. Masquerading as Lamonay, an elderly, hooded Bajoran, he murders the clone of himself that he created to frame Odo for his murder, in a plot to seek vengeance. ("A Man Alone")

IBUDAN CLONE # 1

Clone of the Bajoran Ibudan, created from a new technique called tri-phasic cloning. He was murdered by Ibudan himself. ("A Man Alone")

IBUDAN CLONE # 2

Another clone of Ibudan, this one created in Dr. Bashir's medical lab from DNA samples in Ibudan's guest quarters. ("A Man Alone")

ICED RAKTAJINO

Beverage served in Quark's. Chilled Klingon coffee. ("The Passenger")

I'DANIAN SPICE PUDDING

Dessert served to Dax in Quark's. Served double whipped. ("Babel")

IDRAN

A ternary star system consisting of twin "O" type companions in the Gamma Quadrant. Closest star system on the opposite end of the Wormhole, less than five light-years away from the mouth. It has no Class M planets. ("Emissary")

ILVIAN MEDICAL COMPLEX

Hospital and research facility located in the North-Eastern district of Bajor. Dr. Surmak Ren is on staff there. ("Babel")

IMAGINATION ALIENS

Advanced life-forms that followed one of the ships through the wormhole and chose to study the humans on DS9. They were fascinated by the imaginations of the crew, and, to study it, allowed everyone's imagination to come true. They appeared in the forms of Buck Bokai, a duplicate Dax, and Rumplestiltskin. ("If Wishes Were Horses")

INFERNITE

An explosive used to blow up the school on DS9. It is common and easily obtained. ("In The Hands Of The Prophets")

INFIRMARY

Medical facility on DS9. ("The Passenger")/("Q-Less") where Dr. Bashir first examines O'Brien for aphasia. ("Babel")

IONIZED L-BAND EMISSIONS

Exhaust products from Tosk's Gamma Quadrant ship and from his pursuer's ship. ("Captive Pursuit")

ISOLINEAR CO-PROCESSOR

Security control panel that Neela and O'Brien repaired together. It affects the weapon detectors on the Promenade. ("In The Hands Of The Prophets")

J

JABARA

Nurse assistant to Dr. Bashir in the infirmary. ("Babel")

JAHEEL, CAPTAIN

Rude, alien, freighter captain that wishes to

break quarantine and leave DS9. He forcibly tries, creating a dangerous situation. He was trying to transport a shipment of Tamen Sasheer to Largo Five before it spoiled. ("Babel")

JAS-GAL

Nog's alien assistant in the break-in to steal ore samples. Possibly working for Quark. He throws a weapon at Odo which sails right through him. ("Emissary")

He is a member of the B'Kaazi race. ("Emissary") (novelization)

JENNIFER SISKO

Beautiful dark-skinned wife of Lt. Commander Benjamin Sisko, serving aboard the Saratoga. Mother of Jake Sisko who was a boy of eleven when she was killed in the Borg massacre at Wolf 359. Benjamin called her Jen, and met her on Gilgo Beach. ("Emissary")

JERADDO

Bajor's fifth moon, and the subject of Bajor's first large-scale energy transfer from the tapping of it's molten core. The habitable moon was supposed to have been evacuated and its 50 inhabitants resettled for the process. However, Mullibok and his two companions refused to leave their home, even though when the moon's core was tapped it would release toxic gases. ("Progress")

JOKARIAN CHESS

Game played by Jadzia Dax. She offers to play Sisko in a game. ("The Nagus")

JONAS, ENSIGN

Engineer assistant to O'Brien. ("The Nagus")

JORANIAN OSTRICH

An animal Odo uses as an example. It hides by sticking its head in the water, sometimes

until it drowns. ("Past Prologue")

JUMJA

Sweet treat sold on a stick by vendors on the Promenade. It is made from the sap of the jumja tree and contains a lot of Vitamin C. Neela had explained about Jumja to O'Brien who now enjoys it. ("In The Hands Of The Prophets")

JURO-COUNTER-PUNCH

Athletic activity sometimes played bare-fisted. Curzon Dax would regularly beat Ben Sisko. ("A Man Alone")

K

KAI

Title of Bajoran spiritual leader. Opaka was Kai when DS9 was abandoned by the Cardassians. ("Emissary")

KAI OPAKA

(Camille Saviola) She leaves Bajor for the first time and flies to DS9 to fulfill the Prophesy. She wants to go through the Wormhole, but she ends up dying on a Gamma Quadrant moon, where the runabout, Yangtzee Kiang crashes. She is brought to life again by a microbe and chooses to remain on the moon to help mediate the war. ("Battle Lines")

KAI TALUNO

22nd century Bajoran leader who's ship was disabled in the Denorios Belt. He claims to have had a vision where the heavens opened up and nearly swallowed his ship. This was the first evidence of the Wormhole. ("Emissary")

KAINON

A Bajoran man who was imprisoned in the holding cell next to Marritza's. He ended up murdering Marritza

If you're going to do pop culture, Star Trek is the closest thing to classical theater. There's nothing else like it. —Rene Auberjonois

because he was a Cardassian. ("Duet")

KAJADA, TY

(Caitlin Brown) Female Kobliad Security Officer who has been pursuing criminal Rao Vantika for twenty years. She eventually captures & kills him. ("The Passenger")

KALEVIAN MONTAR

Game Odo and Gul Dukat played once in which Odo caught Dukat cheating. ("Duet")

KALLA-NOHRA SYNDROME

Rare disease caused by a mining accident at Gallitepp, a Bajoran forced labor camp. Only people present at that time could contract it. Aamin Marritza had it when he arrived on DS9. Kalla-Nohra is chronic and requires medication. ("Duet")

KALEANS

Race of people that cornered Curzon Dax and Sisko on Rochani Three. ("Dramatis Personae")

KANDIPPERS

Possibly some small Bajoran aquatic animal. Mullibok uses the term in a saying: "like spearing kandippers in a bottle." ("Progress")

KARO-NET TOURNAMENT

Possibly a sporting event Odo mentions as an example of what men like to watch. ("A Man Alone")

KATTERPOD BEANS

Crop grown on Jeraddo by Mullibok and his companions. Apparently chlorobicrobes sprayed in the soil make them grow better. ("Progress")

KAVAL

Minister of State of Bajor. He was very interested in the dealings with Cardassian war

criminals like Marritza. ("Duet")

KEE-BHOR

Medical officer aboard the Klingon ship Toh'Kaht before it blew up. ("Dramatis Personae")

KEENA

(Annie O'Donnell) Old female Bajoran living on Jeraddo who refused to leave during the Bajoran evacuation. Her companions, Mullibok and Baltrim also refused to leave. Keena, along with Baltrim, was rendered speechless by the Cardassians during their oppression of Bajor, 18 years previous. Soon after they escaped to Jeraddo. Because of the Cardassians, they fear people in uniform. They were removed forcibly. ("Progress")

KEIKO'S MOTHER

Mother to Keiko O'Brien. She lives in Kumomoto, on Earth.

("Emissary") Keiko's Mother is visited by the O'Brien's on her 100th birthday. ("Dax")

KELTON FOUR

Planet where Dax once helped the Federation deliver rain-inducing technology. ("Dramatis Personae")

KELLIPATES

Possibly a Bajoran flower. A tree in Kira's yard blocked out the sun for her Kellipates. ("Progress")

KIRA NERYS, MAJOR

(Nana Visitor) First Officer of DS9 and the attache' assigned to the station by the Bajoran Provisional government as the Bajoran representative. Second in command of the space-station. She claims that she has a bad habit of telling the truth. Originally, Kira was very hostile to the thought of the Federation and Bajorans working together on DS9, but

To play a strong woman on television, or in any medium, really, is un-usual, very rare, and it's a huge joy for me. -- Nana Visitor

she doesn't always see eye-to-eye with the Bajoran provisional government. She has been fighting for Bajoran independence since she was old enough to pick up a phaser. Kira learned to do what was needed in the refugee camps, and served with Tahna Los in the Bajoran underground. Now she claims she is serving on DS9 to fight for Bajor in her own way. ("Past Prologue")

Kira claims her relationship with Sisko is like mixing oil and water, yet she respects Odo's opinion. She still has nightmares about her involvement in the raids on the Haru outposts. She is not proud of her actions. ("Past Prologue")

Kira can be easily angered, ("Move Along Home") and often goes to extremes, including kidnapping Dr. Surmak, to help find a cure for the aphasia virus. ("Babel")

She is quite upset when she discovers a Cardassian file classifying her terrorist activities as "A minor operative who's activities are limited to running errands for the terrorist leaders." Kira breaks down when the Kai is killed and begins a Bajoran death chant. Opaka had always been a symbol of hope to Kira. Opaka convinces her to accept the violence inside her so she can move beyond it, but she's afraid the Prophets won't forgive her for her violent life since childhood. ("Battle Lines")

Kira, while on Jeraddo, befriends Mullibok, a Bajoran who refuses to leave his home. He gets to her by bringing out her past and comparing her tactics to the Cardassians. As a result, she tones down her efforts and sympathizes with him, but eventually she orders security to forcibly remove him.

Then, softening up again, she jeopardizes her career to protect Mullibok and his right to stay. But eventually, after talking to Sisko, she decides to do her duty and forcibly removed Mullibok by burning down his cottage and beaming him up to a Runabout. She doesn't like to be called girl. Her father wasn't a farmer, but he knew how to grow better Katterpod beans. ("Progress")

Despite her tough exterior, she does harbor Bajoran religious beliefs, proved when she defends Vedek Winn's charge of blasphemy in the school. Eventually she saw how Vedek Winn manipulated people to plot the assassination of Vedek Bareil and confronted her angrily. Kira once envied Vedek Winn because her faith was so strong. ("In The Hands Of The Prophets")

She was a member of the Shakaar resistance group on Bajor against the Cardassians. She helped liberate Gallitepp. Kira was 12 when she started fighting and didn't keep count of how many Cardassians that she killed. ("Duet")

KLAESTRON FOUR

Nearby world to DS9 where Dax is wanted for murder. Ilon Tandro is from Klaestron Four which is home to a humanoid species with ridged ears. Thirty years previous, it was engaged in a civil war. The Klaestron and Bajorans do not get along because the Klaestrons are long time allies of the Cardassians. So the Bajorans and Klaestrons have no extradition treaties between the worlds. However, the Federation and the Klaestron's do have a treaty. ("Dax")

KLINGON EMPIRE

Leadership body and holdings of the Klingon

race. It is allied with the Federation. ("Dramatis Personae")

KLON PEEGS

Highly sought after sticks in the Wadi culture. They supposedly have many different uses. ("Move Along Home")

KOBHEERIAN

Race that owned the freighter Rak-Miunis that docked at DS9 carrying a Cardassian passenger ill with Kalla-Nohra syndrome. ("Duet")

KOBLIAD

A dying humanoid race which requires the scarce substance deuridium to stabilize their cell structure and prolong their life. ("The Passenger")

KOHLANESE STEW

A dish served in Quark's ("Babel")

KOHN-("A Man Alone")

Bajoran guerilla terrorist warfare group of which Tahna Los is a member. ("Past Prologue")

KOLOS

(Tom McCleister) Tall prunefaced alien friend of Quark's. He is a wealthy collector of antiques and was invited to Quark's and Vash's auction. He purchased the statue from the Verath system for 36 bars of gold-pressed latinum. He has six fingers on his hands. ("Q-Less")

KOR

One of two Bajoran men that Tahna Los conspired with. ("Past Prologue")

KORA TWO

Planet where the Cardassian Marritza was instructor of filing at a military academy. ("Duet")

KORRIS ONE

Quark has a bottle of champagne from this

planet that he offered to Dr. Bashir. ("A Man Alone")

KRAN TOBAL PRISON

(Also spelled Kran-Tobol) Penitentiary on Bajor ("Babel") where Quark has friends and where Ibudan was imprisoned. ("A Man Alone")

KRAUS FOUR

Planet where some lingerie sold in Garak's Promenade shop comes from. ("Past Prologue")

KRAX

Ferengi son of the Grand Nagus Zek, who, with the help of Quark's brother, Rom, tries to assassinate Quark when he becomes Grand Nagus, feeling that the position should have gone to him. ("The Nagus")

KUMOMOTO

Earth home of Keiko O'Brien's mother. ("Emissary")

KYUSHU, U.S.S.

One of 35 Federation ships destroyed at the Wolf 359 Borg massacre. ("Emissary") (novelization)

L

LAMONAY S.

An elderly, hooded Bajoran, who in reality, when unmasked, is Ibudan. He used this alias to kill his clone and frame Odo for murder. ("A Man Alone")

LANGOUR

Special pink beverage Quark uses for business occasions. It is a rare, soothing Cardassian drink. ("Vortex")

LANTAR NEBULA

Nebula which is home to the Sampalo Relic on Hoek Four, and is a place where Q wished to take Vash. ("Q-Less")

My father had a voice that shook the walls like thunder. He sang for a very famous gospel group named Wings Over Jordan. My mother was a pianist, organist, choral conductor and one of the first black women to get a master's degree in music from Northwestern. My uncle was one of the original Delta Rhythm Boys.—Avery Brooks

LAPOLIS SYSTEM

Star System where the Enterprise was ordered to go after briefing Sisko. ("Emissary")

LARGO FIVE

Destination of alien Captain Jaheel and his shipment of Tamen Sasheer. ("Babel")

LARISH PIE

Food served during negotiations between the Paqu and the Navot. Supposedly the Cardassians replicators make it very well. ("The Storyteller")

LAROSIAN VIRUS

Disease Dr. Bashir thinks Jadzia must have when she tries to seduce him. ("If Wishes Were Horses")

LASUMA

Place on the planet Bajor that is home to a grain-processing center. ("Dramatis Personae")

LATINUM

Valuable metal element which is an intricate part of the currency gold-pressed latinum. It can also be used independently in jewelry, such as in Lwaxana Troi's brooch. ("The Forsaken")

LAURIENTO

Massage holo-program number 1-O-1-A that Ibudan used in the holosuite before he was killed. ("A Man Alone")

LEVEL FOUR CLEARANCE

Security rating Quark achieves using his illegally obtained security rods. ("Vortex")

LEVEL 5, SECTION 3

Located in DS9 in the Habitat Ring, it is where the weapons are stored. It is restricted to Security level seven and above. ("Captive Pursuit")

LEVEL FIVE SECURITY PROTOCOL

Top security code only given to Odo and Sisko. ("Dramatis Personae")

LISSEPIAN

Race of the freighter captain that buys the Yamok sauce from Nog and Jake. ("Progress")

LISSEPIAN FREIGHTER CAPTAIN

Commander of a ship that purchased Yamok sauce from Nog and Jake. He will probably turn around and sell it to the Cardassians that he deals with. He trades 100 gross of self-sealing stem bolts that he was stuck with when a Bajoran couldn't pay. ("Progress")

LOCATOR BOMB

A glowing sphere-shaped Ferengi weapon which locks onto its target's pheromones. It is made up from Sorium and Argine, Ferengi explosives. ("The Nagus")

LOCUTUS

(Patrick Stewart) Borg entity who served as spokesman at the battle of Wolf 359. Locutus was really the altered Captain Jean-Luc Picard of the Starship Enterprise with Borg implants such as a prosthetic eye, sensor scope and a mechanical arm attachment. A machine hybrid of Picard and Borg. ("Emissary")

LOJAL

Male Vulcan Federation Ambassador who visits DS9 for a fact-finding mission concerning the wormhole. He was saved by Dr. Bashir in a DS9 corridor fire. ("The Forsaken")

LOKAR BEANS

Ferengi appetizers served in Quark's. ("Move Along Home") He has a large stock of the beans. ("Progress")

LONDON KINGS

Baseball team the legendary Buck Bokai played for in the 2342 season. ("If Wishes Were Horses")

LURSA

Klingon woman of the House of Duras. Sister of B'Etor. Arrived on DS9 after trying to gain power of the Klingon High Council, which resulted in a brief civil war. Until their DS9 arrival, the renegade sisters were in hiding. They came to DS9 to get a payment from Tahna Los. (Also see ST:TNG episode "Redemption" and DS9 episode "Past Prologue")

LUSSILLA

Woman mentioned by Mullibok in his sleep. She was obviously someone he was protecting from harm. ("Progress")

LUTA

Student in Keiko's school. ("The Nagus")

They put me through a lot of hoops to get the part. I went back four or five times to convince them I was the actor—they were looking for actors for all the parts in London, New York, and everywhere! —Rene Auberjonois

M

MAGISTRATE

Title given to Faren Kag, leader of the Bajoran village of the Sirah and the legendary Dal'Rok beast-cloud. ("The Storyteller")

MAIHAR'DU

Hupyrian servant to the Grand Nagus. He did not show up at Zek's funeral. He taught Zek a Dolbargy sleeping trance to fake death. ("The Nagus")

MAJUT

Second in command to Cardassian commander Gul Jasad. ("Emissary") (novelization)

MARALTIAN SEEV-ALE

Beverage secured from Quark by Odo and served to Kira to console her. ("Duet")

MARIAH FOUR

Planet visited by the Valerian ship Sherval

Das. It is one of the stops the Valerians use to secure dolamide. ("Dramatis Personae")

MARRITZA, AAMIN
(Harris Yulin) Cardassian with Kalla-Nohra syndrome that arrives on DS9 on a Kobheerian freighter. He was an instructor at a military academy on Kora Two for the previous five years. Before that, he claims he was a file clerk at Gallitepp for 14 units of service where he received numerous commendations. Because of the guilt he suffered for his small role on Gallitepp, he altered his face to impersonate Gul Darhe'el, its leader. He was stabbed to death by an angry Bajoran, Kainon, on the Promenade. He was never on any list of Cardassian war criminals ("Duet")

MASTER SURCHID
Title for the leader of the Wadi. Falow currently holds this position. ("Move Along Home")

McCOULLOUGH, CAPTAIN
Wrote the revised first-contact procedures for Starfleet. ("Move Along Home")

MELBOURNE, U.S.S.
Federation starship destroyed by the Borg at the battle of Wolf 359. Lt. Commander Benjamin Sisko witnessed its destruction. ("Emissary") (novelization)

MESON
Warp eddies of Starfleet power reactors have meson particle emissions. ("Battle Lines")

MICROBE
Specific biomechanical environmental artificial micro-organism, similar to a nanite, which restores the body

to life on the penal colony moon in the Gamma Quadrant. The body becomes permanently dependent on the microbes for all cellular functions. Also, once one leaves the moon, they would quit functioning, leaving the person dead. ("Battle Lines")

MINISTER

Title of Trill representative, Selin Peers. ("Dax")

MINISTER OF STATE

Bajoran Governmental official. The current Minister is Kaval. ("Duet")

MINISTERS

Members of the Bajoran Provisional Government who have voting privileges. ("Past Prologue")

MIRADORN

Race of a pair of raiders who visit DS9. The twins Rok-Kel and Ah-Kel are part of a unique species where the two function as one being. They are said to be a quarrelsome people. ("Vortex")

MISSION RECORDER

Similar to aviation's flight recorder, it provides insight into the destruction of a ship. It emits a transponder signal. ("Dramatis Personae")

MISZINDOL ORE

(Script spelling: Miszinite Ore) Rich deposits of this lucrative substance can be found on Stakoron Two in the Gamma Quadrant. ("The Nagus")

MODELA APERTIF

A bright and sweet 3 layered (blue being the top layer) drink served to Dax in Quarks. ("Dramatis Personae")

MODULATED PARTICLE BEAM

Scanning device from the Gamma Quadrant

ship that pursued Tosk. ("Captive Pursuit")

MONKS

Bajoran religious members who study the Orbs or Tears of the Prophets. ("Emissary")

MORN

Huge long-faced alien in every bar scene. (His name, given to him by the crew is a scrambled version of NORM, taken from "Cheers" barfly, Norm Peterson.) He laughs when Quark tells him a joke, and shows up when Quark's is closed up for a private party. ("The Nagus") He told Odo of Quark's dealings with Croden, ("Vortex") and once invited Dax to dinner. ("Progress")

MOUDAKIS

Computer readout shows a scheduled lunch between Ibudan and this person. ("A Man Alone")

MULLIBOK

(Brian Keith) Old male Bajoran who refuses to leave his home during the evacuation of Bajor's moon, Jeraddo. He has lived there for forty years and claims he would rather die than leave. He tell tales of how he tamed the place after his escape from Bajor and a Cardassians work camp. To escape, he stowed away on board a Cardassian survey vessel, and claims he overpowered six Cardassians and stole what he needed to start a life on the moon. He suffered a punctured peritoneum when defending Baltrim and Keena from Kira's security forces. Eventually, after Kira forcibly destroys his cottage, she evacuates him. He is a farmer who grows Katterpod beans. He also likes to tell tall tales. ("Progress")

He [Avery Brooks] walks onto the sound stage and he knows everyone's name, first and last, and that's a big crew, a big company, and he knows the guest stars' names. He's such a gentleman. He's wonderful with his children, we see them when they come to the set. I have the utmost respect for him. —Nana Visitor

MULZIRAK TRANSPORT

Ship Vash booked passage on to leave DS9. ("Q-Less")

MUNDAHLA

Home of the Stardancers, it is based in the Teleris cluster. It is also where Q wishes to take Vash to visit. ("Q-Less")

MYRMIDON

Planet where Vash is wanted dead for stealing the Crown of the First Mother. ("Q-Less")

N

NAGUS

Title of the Ferengi leader. Currently it is Zek. Quark was temporarily named Nagus during Zek's fake death. ("The Nagus")

NANITE

Biomechanical artificial micro-organism. ("Battle Lines")

NAVA

Ferengi merchant who was congratulated by the Nagus for his take-over of the Arcybite mining refineries in the Clarius System. He is tired of gouge-mining and wants the opportunity to introduce synthale to the Gamma Quadrant. He agrees to split the profits with Quark, 50-50. ("The Nagus")

NAVOT

Bajoran clan that shares a rivalry with fellow Bajoran clan, the Paqu. Woban is their leader. ("The Storyteller")

NEELA

(Robin Christopher) A Bajoran engineering apprentice who works closely with O'Brien. ("Duet") She was in cahoots with Vedek

Winn in a plot to kill Vedek Bareil. She sacrificed her life and freedom because Vedek Winn convinced her that that's what the prophets wanted. Neela was the one that introduced O'Brien to the Bajoran sweet treat, a Jumja stick. According to O'Brien, she is a really good engineer, even able to teach him things. ("In The Hands Of The Prophets")

NEHELIK PROVINCE

Section of the Planet Rahkar in the Gamma Quadrant, commanded by Exarch Hadran. ("Vortex")

NEHRU COLONY

Nearby colony to DS9. It has a transmitter array that DS9 can link into. ("The Forsaken")

NEUTRINO DISTURBANCES

Over the years, 23 reports of severe neutrino disturbances were detected in the Denorios Belt. ("Emissary") Elevated neutrino levels indicate Wormhole activity. ("Captive Pursuit")

NEW FRANCE COLONY

Nearby colony to DS9. It has a transmitter array that DS9 can link into. ("The Forsaken")

NEWSOM, EDDIE

Buck Bokai remembers hitting a squeaker that went under his glove in a baseball game in the past. ("If Wishes Were Horses")

NINTH RULE OF ACQUISITION

"Opportunity plus instinct equals profit." Part of the Ferengi code. ("The Storyteller")

NOG

(Aaron Eisenberg) Small Ferengi boy, nephew of Quark. He was caught stealing ore samples with the help of Jas-Gal, an alien. He was thrown into the Brig by Sisko. ("Emissary")

Once becoming friends with Jake Sisko, they get into mischief together, since they are the only two close to each other's age. ("A Man Alone")

He taught Jake Sisko about women. ("Move Along Home")

Nog often lies, including telling O'Brien that the Vulcans stole his homework. When Nog is pulled out of school by his father, Jake tutors him because Nog can't read. ("The Nagus")

He likes humanoid women, specifically, he finds Varis Sul, the 15 year-old Tetrarch of the Bajoran Paqu clan, interesting. He is constantly nervous and tongue-tied around her. To show off, he attempts to steal Security Chief Odo's sleeping bucket. Nog thinks baseball is a stupid game and doesn't like playing it with Jake. ("The Storyteller")

Together with Jake, he used his Ferengi profit-making skills to trade Yamok sauce for self-sealing stem bolts, then the stern bolts for land on Bajor, which he sold to his uncle Quark for 5 bars of gold-pressed latinum. Together, he and Jake formed a small company called Noh-Jay Consortium. Quark had to warn Nog about picking up his father's habits, namely replacing a spilled drink without charging for it. ("Progress")

NOH-JAY CONSORTIUM

Name given by Nog and Jake for their fictional company, which they used to trade land for their self-sealing stem bolts. They eventually received seven tessipates of Bajoran property which they sold to Quark for five bars of gold-pressed latinum. ("Progress")

NOL-ENNIS

Humanoid people at war with the Ennis on a

[Rosalind's] great to work with. There really wasn't much time to develop a relationship, to sit at a table and rehearse. We just seemed to click from the beginning. —Colm Meany

penal colony in the Gamma Quadrant. They can never die, thanks to a bio-mechanical presence, and they can never leave the colony, even though they have been there for an eternity. The leader of the Nol-Ennis is Zlangco. ("Battle Lines")

NORIC

One of two Bajoran men that Tahna Los conspired with. ("Past Prologue")

NORKOVA, U.S.S.

Federation ship that carried the deuridium shipment from the Gamma Quadrant to DS9. It carried 12 crew members. ("The Passenger")

NURSE JABARA

Assistant to Dr. Bashir in the infirmary. ("Babel")

O

O'BRIEN, KEIKO

(Rosalind Chao) Wife of Chief of Operations, Miles O'Brien and mother to two year-old Molly. Her mother lives in Kumomoto. ("Emissary")

After a brief time on the station, and hating the environment, Keiko, in an argument, claims that her husband made the decision to transfer there, and she was asked to agree to it instead of deciding together. ("A Man Alone")

She is a botanist and also served aboard the Enterprise She claims she just needs to be useful so when she sees kids on the station getting into trouble, she starts a school. ("A Man Alone")

She took a leave of absence to visit her mother on Earth to celebrate her 100th birthday, ("Dax") and remained on Earth temporarily, leav-

ing her husband in charge of the school. ("The Nagus") She may have a touch of jealousy over her husband Miles because she once teased him about his pretty female assistant Neela. When confronted by Vedek Winn in her classroom concerning her teaching blasphemous material to students, Keiko stubbornly refused to back down, claiming she only teaches science. Keiko doesn't like Jumja sticks because they are too sweet. ("In The Hands Of The Prophets")

O'BRIEN, MILES EDWARD

(Colm Meaney) Chief Operations Officer and Starfleet officer, formerly stationed on and transferred from the U.S.S. Enterprise. He beamed down from his favorite station, Transporter Room Three. ("Emissary")

He has a wife Keiko on board, and a two year-old daughter, Molly. His wife claims that he made the decision to come to DS9 and asked her to agree. He says that they made the decision together. ("A Man Alone")

At one time, O'Brien takes a leave of absence to accompany Keiko to Earth for her mother's 100th birthday party. ("Dax")

While Keiko temporarily remained on Earth, O'Brien fills in as substitute teacher. ("The Nagus") O'Brien is ingenious and inventive. He developed a differential magnetamer to search for and rescue a stranded Sisko and Runabout crew. ("Battle Lines")

O'Brien finds Dr. Bashir irritating and does his best to avoid working with him on a mission. He was chosen by the Bajoran Sirah, to succeed him, and tell the story that would ward off the evil Dal'Rok. But he fails, like the Sirah planned. It is

pointed out that Bashir outranks O'Brien. ("The Storyteller")

O'Brien is known on DS9 as the fix-it man, unfortunately, he was the first one affected by the speech- confusion virus. When extremely busy, he gets irritable and occasionally wishes he had transferred to a Cargo Drone. "No people, no complaints," he says. ("Babel")

O'Brien befriends the Tosk from the Gamma Quadrant, and does everything in his power to help him, even disrupting the station and almost becoming a fugitive himself. Sisko reprimands him for ignoring his duty to Starfleet, ignoring the Prime Directive, and taking off his communicator badge to avoid communications. O'Brien carried a phaser to investigate Tosk's ship, and says he needs eight hours of sleep a night. ("Captive Pursuit")

Rumplestiltskin claimed that O'Brien was afraid of him, but O'Brien responded by saying that he is afraid of no-one. ("If Wishes Were Horses") O'Brien points out that the Cardassians-built computer on board DS9 is his arch-enemy, but when an alien computer system is downloaded, it acts like a stray puppy and wants O'Brien around all the time. Ingeniously, O'Brien builds a computer 'doghouse' to keep it occupied. ("The Forsaken")

Being a true Starfleet Engineer, he claims that he doesn't misplace his tools, and grows very concerned when one turns up missing. His temper can flair proven by his near attack on a Bajoran vendor who refused to sell to him because of his wife's teachings. O'Brien likes the Bajoran sweet treat Jumja sticks. ("In The Hands Of The Prophets")

My parents wanted to see if I was really serious about becoming an actor, so I became an apprentice at a theater in Stratford, Connecticut. They asked John [Houseman] to see if I had any talent, feeling that I was at an age to be easily influenced—away from the business—if I had no talent. But John told them, 'Your son is an actor.'
—Rene Auberjonois

O'BRIEN, MOLLY

(Hana Hatae) Two year-old ("Emissary") (novelization) daughter of Keiko and Miles O'Brien. ("A Man Alone")

She apparently had her third birthday aboard DS9 since she was 3 during the Nagus' visit. ("The Nagus")

O-D-N ACCESS:

O'Brien complained about the Cardassians who built DS9, when he couldn't find the O-D-N access. ("Emissary")

ODO

(Rene Auberjonois) Constable in charge of security on DS9, both during the Cardassian occupation and during the Federation's time. Odo is a shape-shifter, able to change his form into a gelatinous mass and back into virtually anything, such as a bag, ("Emissary") a rat, ("Past Prologue") a chair, ("A Man Alone") a picture, ("Captive Pursuit") a goblet, ("Vortex") a food-service cart ("Babel") etc. although he tries to appear human. He has known Quark on DS9 for nearly four years, in a very antagonistic relationship and still regards him as a thief, although unable to prove it. Odo was found in the Denorios Belt and doesn't know where he came from, and has no idea if there are any others like him. ("Emissary") He claims that he has a hard time creating a humanoid nose. ("Past Prologue")

Odo can't understand the humanoid need to 'couple,' and has never done so himself. He chooses not to because there are too many compromises. ("A Man Alone")

He doesn't allow weapons on the Promenade, ("Emissary") but can get physically violent. He believes in justice, but occasionally he has conflicts about how that justice is to be distributed. Odo is con-

sidered by many to be the most honorable man on the station. Odo needs to return to his natural liquid state every 18 hours. He regenerates in a pail in the back of his office. He claims that he has about 500 enemies who might want to frame him. ("A Man Alone")

Odo likes his privacy and being alone. Odo needs clear jurisdiction over Security or he would resign. ("The Passenger")

Despite his dislike for Quark, Odo slides under a door and saves the Ferengi. ("The Nagus")

When tempted by the bogus information that more shape- shifters exist in the Chamra Vortex in the Gamma Quadrant, Odo person- ally agrees to return the criminal Croden to his planet Rahkar for pun- ishment. He reluctantly believes Croden only when he produces a shape-shifting stone. After Croden saves

Odo's life, Odo returns the favor and allows he and his daughter to escape. He calls the shape-shifting stone 'cousin' and fondly wish- es he could find his home. When Odo visits Quark's, "the usual" for him is nothing. ("Vortex")

Odo cannot under- stand the humanoid obsession with accumu- lating wealth and pos- sessions. He claims he needs nothing more than his work. ("Q-Less")

Odo was sent to Klaestron Four by Sisko to investigate the mur- der of General Tandro, supposedly by Dax. ("Dax")

The aphasia virus doesn't seem to affect him. Odo never both- ered to learn how to gamble, even though he spends lots of time in Quark's. ("Babel")

He claims that no one will ever take one of his prisoners as long as he's alive. Odo refuses

to use a phaser. ("Captive Pursuit")

Odo is the only one not affected by the mutiny condition brought back from the Gamma Quadrant. Dr. Bashir can't analyze or treat Odo. He is just too different, for example, he doesn't have a humanoid brain. Only Odo and Sisko have top Level Five Security Protocol rights. ("Dramatis Personae")

Odo doesn't eat, he doesn't have a real mouth just an approximation. He also has no esophagus, digestive track, or stomach. He is very uncomfortable with the affections of Lwaxana Troi. In fact, he does everything possible to avoid her. When trapped in Turbolift Four with Lwaxana, he can't shapeshift his way out because of the Cardassian turbolift technology which uses exposed Multi-phased currents. Odo shares his private life with her. He tells her that, after he was found, he grew up in a Bajoran research laboratory. He claims he was self-sufficient, but he resents how others abused him, making him perform his shapeshifting talents for their amusement, including transforming himself into a chair and a razorcat. After his 16 hour cycle, Odo needs to regenerate and had to resort to reverting to his liquid state in Lwaxana's pocket. He has no time for romance. Odo's hair is not real, after a lot of practice, he imitated the hairstyle of the Bajor man that was assigned to him. ("The Forsaken")

Odo has no sense of smell, and Quark claims he has no imagination, but Odo proves him wrong when he imagines Quark in the brig. ("If Wishes Were Horses")

He has little tolerance for the Bajoran belief in the Prophets.

Nana has explained that the only way she felt she could identify with the pain in Major Kira's life was due to her own experience in going through childbirth.
"Freedom fighter, nothing! Give birth!"

("In The Hands Of The Prophets")

Odo has all the lists for Cardassian War criminals and he used to play Kalevian Montar with his former commander, Gul Dukat, until he caught the Cardassian cheating. ("Duet")

ODO'S OFFICE

Located on the Promenade, it's where he keeps his regenerative pail. ("A Man Alone")

OO-MOX

The sexual stimulation of the Ferengi's ears. Vash apparently possesses quite a talent. ("Q-Less")

OPAKA

Bajoran spiritual leader known as the Kai. She lives in seclusion and rarely sees anyone. She told Sisko that he was to be the Emissary to the Prophets. ("Emissary")

OPAKA, KAI

(Camille Saviola) She leaves Bajor for the first time and flies to DS9 to fulfill the Prophesy. She wants to go through the Wormhole, but she ends up dying on a Gamma Quadrant moon, where the runabout Yangtzee Kiang crashes. She is brought to life again by a microbe and chooses to remain on the moon to help mediate in the war. ("Battle Lines")

OPS

Main operation center on DS9. ("Emissary") Ops, short for Operations, is the command center of DS9. ("The Forsaken")

ORDER

Cardassian Guard. Title preceded by the number, for example, the Seventh Order. ("Emissary")

ORBS

Also known as the Tears of the Prophets. They are glowing devices

housed in jeweled cases that have the power to send one out of 'linear time' and make all of one's memories, the present. Nine of these Orbs had appeared in the skies of Bajor over the previous ten-thousand years. The Cardassians took eight. They were apparently sent by the Prophets from the Celestial Temple to teach the Bajorans and shape their theology. At least five of them were found in the Denorios Belt. ("Emissary")

A fragment is used in the Sirah's green bracelet and transforms the villager's fears into physical form—a storming cloud creature. ("The Storyteller")

ORE SAMPLES:

What Nog and Jas-gal were after when they were caught stealing. ("Emissary")

P

PAD C

Docking pad in the DS9 Station. ("Emissary")

PAGH

Bajoran spiritual life-force, or soul. Can be felt by the Kai holding ones ear. It is replenished by the Prophets. ("Emissary")

PAIL

Where Odo returns to every 18 hours in order to regenerate in his natural liquid state. ("A Man Alone")

PAQU

Bajoran clan lead by a 15 year-old girl, Tetrarch Varis Sul, who are rivals of fellow clan, the Navot. The Paqu try to avoid contact with outsiders. ("The Storyteller")

PAQU/NAVOT TREATY

Ninety year old agreement between rival

Bajoran clans that states: "The border separating the Paqu and the Navot shall forever be the river Glyrhond." The only problem is that the Cardassians diverted the river and altered the boundary. The feud was finally resolved when the land was returned in exchange for free trade access to both sides of the river. ("The Storyteller")

PAULEY, ENSIGN

DS9 Crewman aboard the Ganges who helped Dax rescue Vash from the Gamma Quadrant. ("Q-Less")

PEERS, SELIN

(Richard Lineback) A representative of the Trill who testifies at Dax's extradition hearing. His title is Minister and his symbiote has had seven hosts. His first host was a woman. ("Dax")

PICARD, CAPTAIN JEAN-LUC

(Patrick Stewart) Commander of the U.S.S. Enterprise, who was captured on Stardate 43997 by the Borg and assimilated by the biomechanical race to become their spokesman, Locutus. Strong proponent of Bajor's admittance into the Federation, Picard had the duty of instructing Sisko on his new command. ("Emissary")

He was a good friend of Vash, because he likes a good challenge. They met on Risa. ("Q-Less")

PENAL COLONY MOON

Prison satellite .35 light years from the Wormhole in the Gamma Quadrant. Its bearing in 229 mark 41. It is a moon with an elaborate security satellite system in orbit. It is home to the Ennis and the Nol-Ennis, a warning group of inmates sent there to battle for an

eternity. No one there can die, thanks to a microbe. The moon is in a binary star system. ("Battle Lines")

PINCH

A bad roll in Dabo, especially when two pinches are showing. ("Move Along Home")

PISTRES

Small denomination of currency. ("Dramatis Personae")

PLEA-BARGAINING

Ferengi legal traditions employed by Sisko for Nog's release. ("Emissary")

POTTRIK SYNDROME

Disease which is a distant cousin to Kalla - Nohra Syndrome. Marritza claimed that he had Pottrik rather than Kalla-Nohra. ("Duet")

PREFECT OFFICE:

Office on DS9 that used to house the Cardassian leader, Gul Dukat. It is elevated from Ops so all others would have to look up with respect. It was first Major Kira's office then Commander Sisko's. ("Emissary")

PRIME ASEMETY

Leader of the Gamma Quadrant's Verath System. The Prime Asemety during the 19th Dynasty was Drolock. ("Q-Less")

PRIME DIRECTIVE

On the Penal Colony moon, Sisko claims that the Prime Directive of non-interference does not apply because the Nol-Ennis and the Ennis have served their time a hundred times over. ("Battle Lines") Because of the Prime Directive, Sisko must turn over Tosk to the hunters, even though he strongly disagrees with their practices. ("Captive Pursuit")

PRIMMIN, LT. GEORGE

(James Lashly) Starfleet Security Lieutenant assigned to

DS9, originally sent to oversee security arrangements for a deuridium shipment. ("The Passenger") He has been a Security Officer for six years. ("Move Along Home")

PROMENADE

Central 'business district' on DS9. Shops such as Quark's operate out of here. According to Odo, weapons are not allowed. ("Emissary") Other shops include a clothing store operated by the Cardassian, Garak, and a Replimat. ("Past Prologue")

It once snowed on the Promenade when the imagination- aliens were on board. Also, Gunji Jackdaws, ostrich-like birds, strolled the corridors during the same period. ("If Wishes Were Horses")

PROMETHEAN QUARTZ

Glowing stone that the Assay Office manag-

er mistook Vash's geode for. ("Q-Less")

PROPHETS

Bajoran religious reference to their almighty beings. Supposedly they reside in the Celestial Temple (later known as the Wormhole) and sent the Bajoran nine orbs, known as the Tears of the Prophets, to teach them. ("Emissary")

PROTON COUNTS

Unusually high proton counts lead Dax and Sisko in the direction of the Wormhole. ("Emissary")

PULSE COMPRESSION WAVE

When directed through the phaser banks, a pulse compression wave can produce a phaser-like blast. ("Emissary")

PULSE WAVE TORPEDO

Type of torpedo used in a failed attempt by a Vulcan science vessel to

We were all growing tired when, all of a sudden, the door burst open to the set and Patrick Stewart, Jonathan Frakes and Brent Spiner danced in singing, 'Good morning! Good morning!' They were working late that night, too, and it was their way of welcoming us and saying, 'You see what you're in for!?' —Rene Auberjonois

seal a rift in space, back in the 23rd century. Two-hundred years later, with improved technology, the same device was used to attempt to save the Bajoran system from a similar rift. ("If Wishes Were Horses")

PUP

O'Brien's nickname for a mysterious probe-type ship from the Gamma Quadrant, made from a corundium alloy that has no communication or science modules, only an extensive computer capacity. The computer programming, when downloaded, develops a fondness for O'Brien, much like that from a stray puppy. Slowly it disables the station, until O'Brien builds a computer dog-house for it. He designs a sub-program called 'Pup' which consists of bi-directional data transfer and monitoring commands, which will keep the computer crea-

ture busy indefinitely. ("The Forsaken")

Q

Q

(John deLancie) Member of the Q Continuum, he is omnipotent, powerful, and a chief tormentor of the Federation, notably Captain Picard and the Enterprise. He is also Vash's friend, although their relationship is rocky recently since she left him. He shows petty jealousy when Vash agrees to a date with Dr. Bashir. He entices Sisko into an image of a boxing ring where Sisko decks him, much to Q's astonishment. He often goes to extremes to prove his point, including covering Vash with boils and crippling her to show that she can't get along without him. He reluctantly parts with Vash and reveals that it

was refreshing to see the universe from her eyes. He is known as the 'God of Lies' on the planet Brax. He calls Sisko, 'Benji.' (Also see ST:TNG episodes: "Encounter At Farpoint," "Q-Pid," "Q-Who," "Deja Q." and "Tapestry," also the DS9 episode "Q-Less")

QUADROS ONE PROBE

Probe launched in the 22nd century to explore the Gamma Quadrant. ("Emissary")

QUARK

(Armin Shimerman) Ferengi who runs Quark's, the gambling establishment on the Promenade of DS9. Considered a 'gambler and a thief' by Odo, but Quark claims he hasn't been able to prove it for four years. Sisko appointed him to be 'community leader' for the Promenade. The Ferengi claims he loves a woman in uniform. He has known Odo for four

years and has a very antagonistic, sparring relationship ("Emissary") with him and is particularly fond of Dax. He doesn't deny he is a crook, or that he is the leader of an 'organization,' supposedly, the local Black Market. ("A Man Alone")

He was working with Vantika in a plot to hijack a shipment of deuridium. ("The Passenger")

His cheating of the Wadi delegation resulted in the temporary abduction of Sisko, Bashir, Dax, and Kira as part of a game. Quark claims he learned his lesson. Quark does have a compassionate streak. He chooses the safer path in the Chula game when he knows Sisko and the others are in peril, and cannot bring himself to sacrifice one. He even breaks down when forced to choose. He spent his life figuring out the odds on all sorts of games, and calls him-

self a gambler. ("Move Along Home")

He was temporarily appointed Grand Nagus, leader of the Ferengi. He once let his cousin Barbo be imprisoned on Tarahong, for selling defective warp drives when he was a co-conspirator. ("The Nagus")

Quark is not above extremely shady deals. While trying to buy stolen merchandise, he and an accomplice faked a robbery causing the death of one of the sellers. Behind the bar, Quark has stashed computer rods that allow him access to high security clearance information. Quark uses his security rods to access Level Five. ("Vortex")

He becomes a friend and business partner with Vash who practically seduces him with her Oo-Mox technique. ("Q-Less") Quark is immune to the aphasia virus, he offers Odo help, telling him they can haggle over a price later. He

served on a Ferengi freighter for eight years, and knows how to operate a transporter. ("Babel")

Not the kindest of bosses, Quark once had a new Dabo girl, Miss Sarda, sign a contract that included sexual favors. Quark sees Tosk, an alien with no vices to exploit, as a challenge, and envies him because he lives the greatest adventure. ("Captive Pursuit")

Sometimes Quark shows great concern like when Odo is knocked unconscious by an alien entity. ("Dramatis Personae")

Eventually he wants to expand the holosuite activities to include family entertainment. When the imagination-aliens were on board, Quark used his thoughts to conjure up a beautiful woman for each arm. ("If Wishes Were Horses")

QUARK'S

Gambling establishment on the Promenade of DS9, forced to stay open by Sisko as a result of plea-bargaining for Nog's release. ("Emissary") It houses games like Dabo, a bar, and activities such as the holo-suites. ("Emissary") Quark claims that "Customer satisfaction is our primary concern." and made his brother Rom, Assistant Manager of Policy and Clientele. ("The Nagus")

According to Bashir, Quark's serves a delicious Coos- coos. ("Q-Less")

The bar was reluctantly allowed to be the site of Dax's extradition hearing. ("Dax")

By using the command level replicators, patrons of Quark's were inadvertently exposed to the aphasia virus. ("Babel")

R

RAHKAR

Planet in the Gamma Quadrant. Home to the Croden. Punishment on the planet for being an enemy of the people, is the death of your family. There are no trials for crimes, only punishment. ("Vortex")

RAK-MIUNIS

Name of the Kobheerian freighter that docked at DS9 carrying Aamin Marritza. ("Duet")

RAKTAJINO

It is the Klingon equivalent of coffee, and is served in the Replimat. It can have the same effect as coffee—keeping one awake. ("Dax") It can be served extra-strong. ("If Wishes Were Horses")

RAMSCOOP

Device on a Federation ship that captures stellar gases

and converts them into usable fuel. ("Captive Pursuit")

RASTIPOD

An animal, usually carnivorous, probably Bajoran. Mullibok teases Kira that she walks like one. ("Progress")

RAZORCAT

Animal Odo shape-shifted into during parties back when he was trying to fit-in in the research center. ("The Forsaken")

RECLAMATION CENTER

Manufacturing complex, used to reclaim old matter and recycle it into new products. Such a plant was to be built on the parcel of land owned by the Noh-Jay Consortium, or Nog and Jake. ("Progress")

REP

Klingon taken prisoner aboard his own ship, the Toh'Kaht shortly

If you look at the pilot for The Next Generation, they make the Ferengi sound as though they might be the new Klingons —Armin Shimmerman

before it was destroyed. ("Dramatis Personae")

REPLICATOR

A device that converts energy to matter using a voice command, used to produce food and supplies. The food distributors at the command levels were responsible for the spread of the aphasia disease because of a device attached to the replicators. The replicators work with the help of a pattern generator and have the capability to screen out viruses. ("Babel")

REPLICATOR CENTER

Place where new parts for ships are replicated. ("Captive Pursuit")

REPLIMAT

Cafeteria-style shop on the Promenade which serves items like Tarkalean tea from replicators. ("Past Prologue") Dax & Bashir use this area along with others

to converse over a late night coffee. ("Dax")

RETINAL SCANNER

For security purposes in the Assay Office, it is equipped with a Cardassian MK-12 with an L-90 enhanced resolution filter. It is operated by a laser-like scan of the eye. ("Q-Less")

REYAB

Name of Kobliad transport ship that carried Ty Kajada and Rao Vantika. ("The Passenger")

RHERN

Computer readout shows a scheduled meeting between Ibudan and this person. ("A Man Alone")

ROCHANI THREE

Planet where Curzon Dax and Sisko were cornered by a party of Kaleans. ("Dramatis Personae")

RIGELIAN FREIGHTER

Ship from Rigel that Odo uses for cover to sneak Croden past Ah-Kel and the Miradorn. ("Vortex")

RIGEL SEVEN

Planet where Vantika took over and purged the entire computer system. ("The Passenger")

RIO GRANDE

One of three Runabout class vessels stationed at DS9. The Rio Grande was used by Sisko & Dax in the discovery of the wormhole. ("Emissary")

It was also used by Bashir and Kira to answer a distress call on the Kobliad ship and used by Vantika in Bashir's body to intercept the Deuridium shipment. ("The Passenger")

NCC-72452 is its ship's identification number. O'Brien & Dax used the Rio Grande to search for the Kai and DS9 crew lost in the Gamma Quadrant. ("Battle Lines")

RISA

Vacation spot considered by Nagus Zek because of the voluptuous females. ("The Nagus")

Planet where Captain Picard and Vash met. (Also see ST: TNG episode "Captain's Holiday" and DS9 episode "Q-Less")

ROKAIN ARTIFACTS

Rare & valuable archaeological treasures found on the planet Tartaras Five. ("Q-Less")

ROK-KEL

(Randy Oglesby) One of the alien Miradorn twins who tried to sell stolen goods to Quark. He is killed during a robbery attempt, and his brother, Ah-Kel swears revenge on his killer, Croden. ("Vortex")

ROLADAN WILD DRAW

Game O'Brien fears playing with Kira because of her aggressive bluffing with the Cardassians. ("Emissary")

ROLLMAN, ADMIRAL

Starfleet Admiral who Kira reports to over subspace, concerning Tahna Los' asylum request. She has grey hair. ("Past Prologue")

ROLLOPED

A way of preparing Azna. ("A Man Alone")

ROM

(Max Grodenchik) A Ferengi pit boss in Quark's casino. ("Emissary")

He is Nog's father and brother of Quark. He didn't care for the idea of Nog attending school, and forbad him to attend at the Nagus' prompting. ("A Man Alone")

When Quark becomes Grand Nagus, he appoints Rom as his bodyguard, because he is the only one Quark can trust. But Rom is actually in cahoots with Krax to kill him. Because of his wonderful treachery, Quark promotes him to Assistant Manager of Policy and Clientele. Rom breaks a cardinal rule of the Ferengi when he returns a lost purse to a woman because he was dazzled by her beauty. ("The Nagus") Rom isn't as cunning as Quark. In trying to defend his brother, he instead incriminates him. ("Vortex") He is considered to be an idiot by Odo. ("Babel")

RUJI SISTERS

Seven foot tall sisters, friends of Curzon Dax, that double-dated with Curzon and Sisko when Sisko was in his twenties. ("A Man Alone")

RUJIAN STEEPLE-CHASE

Curzon Dax and Ben Sisko attended its running and double-dated with seven foot Ruji sisters that Curzon knew. ("A Man Alone")

RUL THE OBSCURE

Blue-hooded alien in the audience at Quark's auction. He purchased a Gamma Quadrant necklace for 151 bars of gold-pressed latinum. ("Q-Less")

ROYAL MUSEUM

Museum on Epsilon Hydra Seven where Vash is banned from. ("Q-Less")

RULES OF ACQUISITION

Ferengi code of (Un)Ethics.
Rule One
"Once you have their money, you never give it back." ("The Nagus")
Rule Six
"Never allow family to stand in the way of opportunity." ("The Nagus")
Rule Seven
"Keep your ears open." ("In The Hands Of The Prophets")
Rule Nine
"Opportunity plus instinct equals profit." ("The Storyteller")

RUMPELSTILTSKIN

Fairy tale dwarf O'Brien tells about to his daughter. He appears on DS9 and makes O'Brien very uneasy. It turns out he is an advanced alien life-form curious to find out about human imagination. ("If Wishes Were Horses")

RUNABOUT CLASS VESSEL

Small ship used in transport around the DS9 space station. The Rio Grande, ("Emissary") The Yangtzee Kiang ("Emissary") and the Ganges ("Past Prologue") are the Runabouts assigned to DS9. ("Past Prologue")

RUPTURE

Space anomaly that is a break in the fabric of space. Marked by increased Thoron emissions in the plasma field, it continues to expand and can engulf a star-system, like the Hanoli system back in the 23rd century. It draws in all the matter from the surrounding space. In the case of the one near DS9, it turns out to be imaginary. ("If Wishes Were Horses")

S

SACRED CHALICE OF RIXX

Lwaxana Troi is the holder of the Chalice. A very prestigious position. ("The Forsaken")

SALTAH'NA

Gamma Quadrant race destroyed by the mutiny caused by the energy spheres. The Saltah'na resided on the fifth planet in their system. ("Dramatis Personae")

SAMPALO RELIC

Object of interest on the planet Hoek Four in the Lantar Nebula. Q

wants to take Vash there. ("Q-Less")

SARATOGA, U.S.S.

Federation starship defeated at Wolf 359, commanded by Captain Storil and First Officer Benjamin Sisko. It was the first Starship to arrive, but it was destroyed. ("Emissary")

SARDA, MISS

(Kelly Curtis) The new red-headed alien Dabo girl at Quark's. According to a contracts she signed unknowingly with Quark, she supposedly owes him sexual favors. The agreement was outlined on page 21, sub-section D, paragraph 12 of her employment contract. ("Captive Pursuit")

SCEPTER

Symbolic stick of the Ferengi Grand Nagus. It appears to be wooden with a gold Ferengi head adorning the top. ("The Nagus")

SCHOOL

Opened by Keiko O'Brien to keep DS9 children out of mischief. The school room is on the Promenade. ("A Man Alone")

There were eleven students in the class when they took a field trip to the grain-processing center at Lasuma. ("Dramatis Personae")

It was also the site of the controversy when Vedek Winn arrived on DS9 and accused Keiko of blasphemous teaching. Later, her followers blew up the school—luckily no one was hurt. ("In The Hands Of The Prophets")

SECTOR ZERO-ZERO-ONE

Earth location. Destination of Borg ship at the battle of Wolf 359. ("Emissary")

SECURITY RODS

Used by Quark to gain information from the computer. They

I've always been a little uncomfortable watching myself. It's hearing your own voice on a tape recorder: it makes you uncomfortable
—Rene Auberjonois

enable him to achieve Level 4 clearance. They are about four inches long and shaped like cylindrical rods. ("Vortex") They can be used in the computer to access Security information up to level Five. ("Babel")

SECURITY SENSOR

Located at the end of the corridor from the docking bay, the force-field-like device screens for weapons. It picks up O'Brien's phaser. When O'Brien increased the output by 200 percent, it stunned the Tosk Hunter when he tried to go through. ("Captive Pursuit")

SELF-SEALING STEM BOLTS

Hardware Nog and Jake acquired 100 gross of, in a trade with a Lissepian freighter captain for Yamok sauce. Even O'Brien doesn't know what they're used for. They eventually trade the stem bolts for

seven tessipates of Bajoran land. ("Progress")

SEM'HAL STEW

Cardassian food eaten by Marritza from the replicator's in the Brig. Yamok sauce is apparently used with it. ("Duet")

SEPULO

Ferengi transport ship. ("The Nagus")

SERENAS

Bajoran musical compositions. ("The Forsaken")

SETLIK THREE MASSACRE

Part of the border wars involving the Cardassians. ("Emissary")

SEVENTH ORDER

Military unit consisting of three ships. Gul Jasad is the commander. ("Emissary")

SEVENTH RULE OF ACQUISITION

Seventh Ferengi economic rule that states: "Keep your ears open." ("In The Hands Of The Prophets")

SHAKAAR

Bajoran resistance group of which Kira was a member. ("Duet")

SHAP

Level in the Wadi game of Chula which has six shaps. Only children enter at the first shap. ("Move Along Home")

SHAPESHIFTERS

Unofficial name given to Odo's race, taken from the fact that they can alter their form to just about anything. ("A Man Alone")

Supposedly no one has ever seen another shape-shifter, until Croden visited DS9 from the Gamma Quadrant planet Rakhar, where he claims that Shapeshifters, called changelings, used to live there, and now reside on a nearby colony. ("Vortex")

SHAPE-SHIFTING STONE

Object found by Croden in the Chamra Vortex in the Gamma Quadrant which can alter its shape, even forming itself into a key. Analysts can compare its molecular structure to only one other thing, Odo himself. In actuality, Odo learns that the stones are bought by Rakhari merchants from off-world traders. Odo refers to it as 'cousin.' ("Vortex")

SHEL-LA, GOLIN

(Jonathan Banks) Leader of the Ennis, a people at war on a penal colony in the Gamma Quadrant. ("Battle Lines")

SHERVAL DAS

Name of the Valerian ship that wished to dock at DS9. Kira was sure it

was carrying dolamide. ("Dramatis Personae")

SIRAH

Leader of a certain clan of Bajoran people. The Sirah has the power to ward off the evil Dal'Rok cloud creature. After the death of the Sirah, O'Brien is proclaimed the new Sirah and must continue the storytelling ritual to ward off the Dal'Rok. The Sirah wears a bright orange robe. Hovath became the newest Sirah. ("The Storyteller")

SIRCO CH'ANO

Bajoran who ordered self-sealing stem bolts from the Lissepian freighter captain, but couldn't afford to pay for them. ("Progress")

SISKO, BENJAMIN, COMMANDER

(Avery Brooks) Starfleet representative and Commander of DS9. He served as First Officer of U.S.S. Saratoga. He failed in his attempt to rescue his wife Jennifer who perished in the Borg massacre at Wolf 359. However his is young son Jake was pulled from the wreckage by Sisko and survived. Sisko's job when assigned to DS9 was to make sure that the Bajorans got ready for admittance into the Federation. At first, he objected to the assignment on DS9, even after being assigned to the Utopia Planitia yards for the previous three years. He met his future wife Jennifer on Gilgo Beach shortly after graduating from Starfleet Academy while waiting for his first posting. His father was a gourmet chef, famous for his Aubergine Stew. Sisko is considered by the Bajorans to be the Emissary to the Prophets, because he discovered the wormhole and convinced the inhabitants to allow passage through it. After making contact with the wormhole inhabitants,

I actually thought I was trying out for a guest spot on an episode because I had asked my agent to get me a spot on STAR TREK about a year ago
—Siddig El Fadil

Sisko changes his mind and chooses to continue as DS9's commander. ("Emissary")

He is a very old and dear friend to Dax but his relationship with her was a little uncomfortable, while dealing with the change of Dax's exterior host. Still, much of the basic comradery remains. His past relationship with Curzon Dax was a close friendship, where Curzon was a mentor and a second father. At the Rujian Steeplechase, when Sisko was in his twenties, he and Curzon Dax double-dated with a pair of seven foot Ruji sisters that Curzon knew. Curzon used to beat him regularly at barefisted Juro-Counterpunch. ("A Man Alone")

Sisko staunchly defends his friend and mentor, Curzon Dax, at his hearing, saying that Curzon nurtured the honor that he has today, and taught him much about life. They had been friends 16-18 years before his death and Curzon taught Sisko, who was an Ensign then, about art, science, and diplomacy. He always warned Sisko about his temper. In fact, Curzon once had to deck Sisko to prevent him from killing an Argosian Lieutenant, who threw a drink in his face. Sisko still has the scar on his lip ("Dax") Ben hadn't worn his dress uniform for three years. ("Move Along Home")

He always tells Jake that they should make friends with other cultures. ("The Nagus")

Ben often plays baseball on the holodeck with Jake. Sisko can lose his temper, proven by the fact that he decked Q when provoked. ("Q-Less") Ben once hit an ambassador he was guiding when the ambassador made advances on a fellow-crew person. ("The Forsaken")

Sisko does not like people going over his head. ("Past Prologue")

He follows the Prime Directive, even though he disagrees with the practices of the hunters of the Tosk. But when O'Brien helps the Tosk escape, Sisko makes a feeble attempt to prevent it, realistically allowing it to happen. ("Captive Pursuit")

However, by claiming that the Nol-Ennis and the Ennis on the penal colony moon had developed into their own culture, he agrees to liberate them. ("Battle Lines")

He arrives on Bajor to try to talk some sense into Kira who is stubbornly protecting Mullibok from evacuation. He confesses that he first thought she was hostile and arrogant, but now admits that he needs her, he likes her, and he considers her a friend. ("Progress")

Ben and Odo are the only ones that have top Level Five Security Protocol rights. ("Dramatis Personae")

Sisko's personal hero was Buck Bokai, the baseball slugger. ("If Wishes Were Horses")

He gets very angry at the Bajorans during their protest sick-out. He emphasizes to Kira that his main goal on DS9 is to build a trusting relationship with the Bajoran's and that he wishes some of that trust and respect was returned. ("In The Hands Of The Prophets")

SISKO'S FATHER

A gourmet chef, his specialty was Aubergine stew. ("Emissary")

He insisted that his family eat together every night and experiment with new recipes on them, calling his family his 'test-tasters.' ("A Man Alone")

SISKO, JAKE (JACOB) ("Emissary") (novelization) (Cirroc Lofton)

Son of Benjamin and Jennifer Sisko. Survived

the massacre at Wolf 359 when his father and Hranok pulled him from his wrecked cabin. Originally he did not want to go to DS9. He often plays baseball or fishes in the holodeck. ("Emissary")

Once becoming friends with Nog, he proceeds to get into a lot of mischief, because they are the only too close to the same age. ("A Man Alone") Jake is 14 ("Move Along Home") Jake likes Bajoran girls and claims he knows about women from Nog. ("Move Along Home")

He also backs up Nog, even in a lie, and chose to hang out with Nog in the cargo bays rather than attend a Bajoran Festival with his father. As it turns out, a good portion of his time was used to help tutor Nog. ("The Nagus")

Jake, further influenced by Nog, ventures into a profit-making scheme with the Ferengi boy in which they trade Yamok sauce for self-sealing stem bolts, then for land on Bajor, and finally for a profit of five bars of gold-pressed latinum. ("Progress")

Jake plays baseball in the Holosuites nearly every afternoon. Jake still tries to get Nog to play baseball, even though he hates it. ("If Wishes Were Horses")

He is angered by the religious bigotry in his school. ("In The Hands Of The Prophets")

Young Sisko has a normal adolescent sexual appetite, shown by his attraction to a 15 year-old girl, Varis Sul, a Bajoran leader, aboard the station. Jake speaks very highly of his father and trusts him. ("The Storyteller")

SIXTH RULE OF ACQUISITION

"Never allow family to stand in the way of opportunity." A part of the Ferengi code. ("The Nagus")

SORIUM

Component of a Ferengi locator bomb. ("The Nagus")

SPEAKER, TRIS

Famous Baseball player from the past Quark mentions, that Jake plays with in the holosuite. ("If Wishes Were Horses")

STADIUS, CAPTAIN

A reception was held for him on DS9. ("If Wishes Were Horses")

STAKORON TWO

Gamma Quadrant world that has rich deposits of the very lucrative miszindol ore. ("The Nagus")

STARDANCERS

Based at Mundahla in the Teleris cluster, they are something Q wishes to take Vash to visit. ("Q-Less")

STARDATE 44002.3

Fleet of forty Federation starships were ordered to Wolf 359 to intercept a Borg vessel on its way to Earth. ("Emissary")

STARDATE 46379.1

Three years after Borg attack. ("Emissary")

STARDATE 46388.2

When Sisko took over DS9. ("Emissary")

STAR DRIFTER

Green drink Kira orders in Quark's. ("The Storyteller")

STARDUSTER

(Or FERENGI STAR-DUSTER) Ferengi drink served in Quark's. It is pink in color. ("Babel")

STASIS ROOM

Scientific and medical room used as a laboratory and morgue. ("The Passenger")

STEAMED AZNA

Food Dax orders in Quarks. Apparently she has been eating it for years and has tried many times to convince Sisko to eat it too. She

claims that it would put years on his life, but Sisko passes on it anyway. ("A Man Alone")

STOL

Ferengi cousin of Quark. He is wealthy enough to by a Gamma Quadrant dagger for 105 bars of gold-pressed latinum. ("Q-Less")

STORIL, CAPTAIN

(John Noah Hertzler) Vulcan Captain of U.S.S. Saratoga. Killed in Borg massacre at 359. ("Emissary")

STORY

Told by the Sirah in a Bajoran village, it keeps away the cloud-entity, Dal'Rok. ("The Storyteller")

SUAREZ, MAGGIE, ENSIGN (April Grace)

Dark-skinned female Transporter Chief on duty in Transporter Room Three, when O'Brien beamed off the Enterprise for DS9.

("Emissary") (novelization)

SUBROUTINE A-N-A

Computer file used by Neela under O'Brien's name in her plot to kill Vedek Bareil. The code to decipher it is 4100 RLX. ("In The Hands Of The Prophets")

SUB-SPACE CROSSOVER SHUNT

Device attached to a secondary unprotected computer system, enabling Vantika to access DS9's computer system. ("The Passenger")

SURAX

A valuable mineral that is used to make jewelry. Quark tries to tempt Odo with a Surax ring. ("Q-Less")

SURMAK REN, DR.

Bajoran doctor and colleague of Dekon Elig, who designed the biomechanical Aphasia device. Surmak witnessed Dekon's death

Cirroc is very much a part of my family. As a matter of fact, people are always asking me, 'Is he your son?' We're that close
—Avery Brooks

and now runs a medical complex on Bajor. He is kidnapped by Kira and forced to help find a cure for the virus. He was a member for 6 months of the Higa Metar sect of the Bajoran Underground and repatriated to Bajor upon closing of the Bellos Seven Internment Camp, on Stardate 46302, where he was held prisoner. When he returned to Bajor he served as Chief Administrator of the Ilvian Medical Complex in Bajor's North Eastern District. ("Babel")

SYNTHALE

Synthetic beverage that has the alcoholic effect that can be easily shaken off. A Ferengi creation. ("Captive Pursuit") The local Bajoran version is described as 'dreadful' by Quark. ("Emissary") Quark serves the Bajoran version during the Paqu/Navot negotiations. ("The Storyteller")

T

TAHNA LOS

Bajoran, who, after being chased by the Cardassians, was rescued when his ship was destroyed. He requested asylum aboard DS9. He and Major Kira fought together in the underground, and the Cardassians claimed he was a criminal. His body is scarred from all the injuries he has suffered as a Kohn Ma terrorist. He continued to perform terrorist acts, even after the Cardassian withdrawal from Bajor. After securing Bilitrium from the Klingon Duras sisters, he attempted to destroy the Wormhole. He was arrested and placed in Federation custody. ("Past Prologue")

TAMEN SASHEER

Cargo of Captain Jaheel's ship destined for Largo Five. It needed to be delivered quickly

before it spoiled. ("Babel")

TAMAMOTA, ENSIGN

(Cassandra Byram) U.S.S. Saratoga's helmsman. She was young and fairly inexperienced, and was killed in Borg massacre at Wolf 359. ("Emissary") (novelization)

TANDRO, ARDELON, GENERAL

Klaestron father of Ilon Tandro. He was murdered 30 years before Dax was arrested for his death. He was killed during the Klaestron civil war where Curzon Dax was the Federation mediator. Tandro and Dax were close friends, and after his death, Tandro, whose troops won the war, was made a national hero. His widow, Enina, defends Dax, claiming that Curzon would never conspire against him. As it turns out, Tandro himself was

the traitor, and the rebels were the ones who killed him. ("Dax")

TANDRO, ENINA

(Fionnula Flanagan) Widow of Klaestron General Ardelon Tandro, who defends Dax against the murder accusations. She admits that Curzon was in love with her and they were having an affair. ("Dax")

TANDRO, ILON

Humanoid alien, special envoy from Klaestron Four, sent to DS9 to extradite Dax for the murder of his father 30 years previous. His mother, Enina, defends Dax. ("Dax")

TANESH POTTERY

A valuable set of pottery that Quark tries to tempt Odo with. ("Q-Less")

TARAHONG

Planet where Quark and his cousin Barbo once sold defective warp drives. The Tarahongians

are very gullible people. ("The Nagus")

TARAHONG DETENTION CENTER

Prison where Quark's cousin Barbo was jailed. ("The Nagus")

TARG

Klingon boar-like creature. While making idle conversation, Quark claims he once sold a whole herd. ("The Storyteller")

TARKALEAN TEA

Claimed to be 'very good' by Doctor Bashir who drank it in the Replimat. ("Past Prologue")

TARTARAN LAND-SCAPES

Quark's art collection that he supposedly shows to his female friends. ("If Wishes Were Horses")

TARTARAS FIVE

Planet where Quark tries to entice Vash to go with him to plunder some Rokain artifacts

from the ruins of the provincial Capital. She decides to go alone. ("Q-Less")

TAXCO

A demanding female Federation ambassador representing the Arbazan race, who visits DS9 on a fact-finding mission, concerning the wormhole. She was saved by Dr. Bashir in a DS9 corridor fire. ("The Forsaken")

TEAR OF THE PROPHET

A glowing orb device, housed in a jeweled case, that sends Sisko, and later Jadzia, into a flashback. It has the power to send one out of linear time and make all of one's memories the present. Nine of these orbs had appeared in the sky's of Bajor over the previous ten-thousand years. The Cardassians took eight. They apparently were sent by the Prophets from the Celestial

Rene is one of the most fun people I've ever met. He's got the best stories; he's a very vibrant, happy soul and we've gone out to dinner, the whole families.
—Nana Visitor

Temple to teach the Bajorans and shape their theology. At least five of the orbs were found in the Denorios Belt. ("Emissary")

TELERIS CLUSTER

Home of the Stardancers at Mundahla. Also a place where Q wanted to take Vash. ("Q-Less")

TEL-PEH, CAPTAIN

Captain of the Klingon ship Toh'Kaht which was destroyed by the mutinous First Officer. ("Dramatis Personae")

TESSIPATE

Unit of measurement for land on the planet Bajor ("Progress")

TETRARCH (also spelled Tetrach)

Title given to a leader of a Bajoran clan. ("The Storyteller")

THALMERITE DEVICE

Name the Klingon's gave the Energy Spheres

in the Gamma Quadrant that caused dissension on their ship. ("Dramatis Personae")

THERMOLOGIST

Type of scientist assigned to Jeraddo to study and plan the tapping of the moon's core for thermal energy. ("Progress")

THETA CLASS

Class of Miradorn vessel flown by Ah-Kel. It is faster and more powerful than a DS9 Runabout. ("Vortex")

THIALO

Consequence of a bad role in the game of Chula. When this occurs, one player must be sacrificed so the others can live. ("Move Along Home")

THORON EMISSIONS

Increased levels in the plasma field cause concern in Ops. The Thoron Emissions are falsely blamed for the

imagination occurrences.

THORON FIELD

Can block scanners from reading the defense system of DS9. ("Emissary")

TOH'KAHT

Name of the Klingon Bird of Prey that returns from the wormhole early and explodes, leaving only one survivor who dies soon after. The ship brought back a disease from the Gamma Quadrant. The ship, with its temporary survivor First Officer Hon- Tihl, was on a routine bio-survey mission. Through ships logs it is discovered that the crew mutinied, thanks to a strange condition contracted in the Gamma Quadrant. Its captain was Tel-Peh, Medical Officer was Kee-Bohr, and a crewperson was called Rep. ("Dramatis Personae")

TOH MAIRE

A volatile pocket of gas that could ignite and blow a ship apart if destabilized. The pockets are located in the Chamra Vortex in the Gamma Quadrant. ("Vortex")

TOLSTOI, U.S.S.

One of 35 Federation ships destroyed at the Wolf 359 Borg massacre. ("Emissary") (novelization)

TORAN

A Bajoran government minister who is adamant about removing the farmers from Bajor's moon, Jeraddo. ("Progress")

TORANIUM

Cardassian metal used in DS9 to line wall and bulk-heads. It is impenetrable by phasers on maximum, but can be cut with a bipolar torch. ("The Forsaken")

TOSK

(Scott MacDonald) Reptilian alien from the Gamma Quadrant. He arrived through the wormhole in a damaged ship. Tosk is befriended by O'Brien who protects him from his pursuers. It is discovered that Tosk is a special life-form bred exclusively to be hunted for sport. The Tosk, a race, is honored by the hunters, and are a symbol of nobility and courage. They can become invisible for short periods of time. Tosk refuses asylum aboard DS9 because it is not honorable. O'Brien calls him 'Friend,' and tells him he is the first visitor from the Gamma Quadrant. When he visits Quark's, the Ferengi is puzzled by the fact that Tosk has no vices to exploit. Tosk explains, "I live the greatest adventure one could ever desire." Tosk only requires 17 minutes of sleep per rotation. And liquid nutrients are stored throughout his body in plasmic fibers. ("Captive Pursuit")

TOSK HUNTER

(Gerrit Graham) Leader of the three hunters of the Tosk. ("Captive Pursuit")

TRACTOR BEAM

Towing device used to save the life and ship of Tosk. ("Captive Pursuit")

T'VRAN

Vulcan science vessel which carried Croden and his daughter Yareth to Vulcan. ("Vortex")

TRANSIT AID CENTER

Run by Zayra, a Bajoran, the center is used by visitors for information and assistance. ("A Man Alone")

TRANSMITTER ARRAY

Network of nearby Colonies that DS9 can link with through subspace. They include Nehru Colony, New France Colony, and

Corado One. ("The Forsaken")

TRANSPONDER

Device inside a mission recorder that emits a signal. ("Dramatis Personae")

TRANSPORTER ROOM THREE

O'Brien's favorite station aboard the Enterprise. He disembarked from there with Captain Picard manning the controls. ("Emissary")

TRICORDER

Scientific tool used to gather information. According to Dr. Bashir, it is very accurate with live subjects but not always accurate with dead ones. ("The Passenger")

TRIDIUM

Toxic gas used in a small quantity by Dax and O'Brien to trace the source of a dangerous particle flow. ("Q-Less")

TRILL

Symbiote, or joined species, of which Jadzia Dax is a member. The worm-like slug is transferred from one humanoid host body to another when the original host body grows old. The symbiote inside continues to live and incorporates the personality and memories of all previous hosts and lives. ("Emissary")

Trills have cold hands, and don't look for romance, in fact they find it quite a nuisance. Although they occasionally do have sexual feelings in their youth, they try to live in a higher plane and rise above those feelings. ("A Man Alone")

Hosts are aware of memories and actions of their previous lives, including those carried by the symbiote humanoids until the early to mid-twenties when they take on the Trill relationship. The humanoid host's mind

does not give way to that of the transferred slug-like symbiote. Instead, they blend or share minds, and consequently, each union develops a new personality. Medically, the Trill slug, and the Trill host are two entirely different persons, with distinctly different brain waves. The slug-like symbiote retains its pattern from host to host. To become a Trill host, one must overcome fierce competition to achieve the great honor. The applicant must win scholarships, and excel at tests of character and psychological stability. After 93 hours, the host and symbiote become biologically interdependent. The Trill has two cerebral nuclei, or two brains that communicate between each other. (Also see ST:TNG episode "The Host" and the DS9 episode "Dax")

TRI-PHASIC CLONING

An experimental cloning process developed by a Bajoran prisoner who was arrested and sent to Kran Tobal prison by the Cardassians for conducting experimental research. ("A Man Alone")

TRITANIUM

Metal, often used in making tools. ("In The Hands Of The Prophets")

TRITANIUM ALLOY

Particles found lodged in dead Klingon Hon-Tihl's chest. ("Dramatis Personae")

TRIXIAN BUBBLE JUICE

A beverage served in Quark's to youngsters. Quark served it to Tetrarch Varis Sul, who was insulted and threw it in his face. ("The Storyteller")

TROI, LWAXANA

(Majel Barrett) Female Federation Betazed Ambassador

who visits DS9 on a fact-finding mission concerning the wormhole. She is the mother of Deanna Troi, the ship's Counselor aboard the U.S.S. Enterprise. She, like all Betazoids, has telepathic powers, but they can't be used on Ferengi or their cousin race, the Dopterian. Upon arrival, her brooch is stolen and Odo recovers it for her, inspiring Lwaxana to her latest cases of infatuation and flirtation. When trapped in Turbolift Four with the Security Chief, she ends up supporting a liquid Odo in her garment as well as comforting him. Her titles are Daughter of the Fifth House, Holder of the Sacred Chalice of Rixx, Heir to the Holy Rings of Betazed. She often wears wigs. She tells Odo of the time she and her daughter were kidnapped by a Ferengi Daimon, and how she made love to him. (Also see TNG Episodes:

"Haven," "Menage A Troi," "Half A Life," "Manhunt" and the DS9 episode "The Forsaken")

TUBE GRUBS
Ferengi wormlike delicacy, served live and chilled. ("The Nagus")

TULAMEK
Part of a Ferengi saying: "The twist of your tulamek." It is equivalent to the saying, "The cut of your jib." ("Dramatis Personae")

TURBOLIFT
Cardassian turbolifts use exposed multi-phased currents, thus preventing Odo from shape-shifting his way out of a stalled lift on DS9. ("The Forsaken")

TURBOLIFT FOUR
Turbolift that Odo and Ambassador Troi were trapped in. ("The Forsaken")

TUROT
Ferengi rival of Hoex, ever since Hoex bought

out his interest in the cargo port on Volchok Prime. ("The Nagus")

TWO-HEADED MAL-GORIAN

Alien that Mullibok knew when he was a boy. Supposedly a two-headed Malgorian can never figure out what it wants to do. ("Progress")

U

ULTIMA THULE

Planet that has a purification plant for dolamide. ("Dramatis Personae")

U.S.S. ENTERPRISE

Starship captained by Jean-Luc Picard who's body was taken over by the Borg and renamed Locutus. ("Emissary")

U.S.S. GAGE

One of the ships destroyed at the battle with the Borg at Wolf 359. ("Emissary")

U.S.S. KYUSHU

One of 35 Federation ships destroyed at the Wolf 359 Borg massacre. ("Emissary") (novelization)

U.S.S. MELBOURNE

Federation starship destroyed by the Borg at the battle of Wolf 359. Lt. Commander Benjamin Sisko witnessed its destruction. ("Emissary") (novelization)

U.S.S. SARATOGA

Federation starship defeated at Wolf 359, commanded by Captain Storil and First Officer Benjamin Sisko. It was the first Starship to arrive, but was destroyed. ("Emissary")

U.S.S. TOLSTOI

One of 35 Federation ships destroyed at the Wolf 359 Borg massacre. ("Emissary") (novelization)

When I read the pilot script of Deep Space Nine I saw this wonderful character; I was very excited. I see a lot of scripts and this was something special.
—Rene Auberjonois

UTOPIA PLANITIA YARDS

Previous three year assignment of Benjamin Sisko before DS9 and after the destruction of the Saratoga. ("Emissary")

V

VADRIS THREE

A charming little world where the natives think they're the only intelligent life in the universe. A place Q wants to take Vash. ("Q-Less")

VALERIAN COMMANDER

(Stephen Park) Commander of the Valerian transport ship, the Sherval Das. ("Dramatis Personae")

VALERIANS

Alien race allied with the Cardassians against the Bajorans. They ran weapons-grade dolamide during the Cardassian occupation of Bajor. Against Kira's wishes, they tried to dock at DS9. Their vessel that wanted to visit DS9 is the Sherval Das. ("Dramatis Personae")

VADOSIA

(Michael Ensign) Overbearing male Bolian Federation Ambassador who visits DS9 on a fact-finding mission concerning the wormhole. He was saved by Dr. Bashir in a DS9 corridor fire. ("The Forsaken")

VANOBEN TRANSPORT

Ship raided two light-years away from DS9. Taken was an egg-like, ahb-jadah bauble, only after two people on board were killed. ("Vortex")

VANTIKA, RAO

A Kobliad diabolical criminal and cold-blooded murderer who was pursued by Ty Kajada for 20 years. After setting fire to his prison cell, he suppos-

edly died of pulmonary trauma. He had been on his way to DS9 to hijack a deuridium shipment when apprehended. Kajada claims he has faked his own death many times. He was a brilliant scientist who killed others to prolong his own life. He used Dr. Bashir's body to store his consciousness in his final attempt to prolong his life. His consciousness was transported to a micro-containment field which was destroyed by Kajada with a phaser. ("The Passenger")

VARIS SUL

(Gina Philips) Leader, or Tetrarch, of the Bajoran clan, the Paqu. She is a 15 year-old girl who becomes friends with the love-struck Nog and Jake. She is very stubborn in getting what she wants for her people. She is an orphan, her parent were killed by Cardassians. She doesn't get a chance to be with people her own age. Her father was a great and strong leader, feared by the Navot, but not afraid to compromise. ("The Storyteller")

VASH

(Jennifer Hetrick) Female maverick archaeologist who recently had been Q's companion until she left him. Also friends with Captain Picard of the Enterprise, who met her on Risa. She had been exploring the Gamma Quadrant with Q for the last two years. According to Quark, Vash possesses a talent for Oo-mox—Ferengi ear-stroking. She deals financially with Quark and agrees to a date with Dr. Bashir. Vash once had her membership from the Daystrom Institute's archaeological council suspended by professor Woo because she puts profit ahead of science every time. Vash hadn't been back to Earth in twelve years. (Also see

ST:TNG episodes "Captain's Holiday" and "Q- Pid") She has been banned from the Royal museum on Epsilon Hydra Seven, is not welcome on Betazed, and is wanted, dead, on the planet Myrmidon for stealing the Crown of the First Mother. She was almost killed on Errikang Seven, and blamed Q. She only accepts payments for her goods in gold-pressed latinum. ("Q-Less")

VAYAN HORN FLIES

Insect-like creature that operate in a swarm. O'Brien uses them as an example. ("Battle Lines")

VEDEK

A high-ranking Bajoran religious official, one step below the Kai. According to Vedek Bareil, there are 112 Vedeks. ("In The Hands Of The Prophets")

VEDEK ASSEMBLY

Governing body on Bajor, consisting of 112 Vedeks. ("In The Hands Of The Prophets")

VEDEK BAREIL (Philip Anglim)

A high-ranking Bajoran religious official. Bareil is a man in his 30's, soft-spoken and gentle. He has the most support in becoming the next Kai and therefore is the target of Vedek Winn's assassination attempt. He also refrains from helping Sisko in solving the Vedek Winn/school crisis because it would hurt him politically; but he does visit DS9 in a good-will gesture. When he was a child, he vowed to get rid of the archaic Bajoran ritual of clasping one's ear to read one's pagh. He began his monastery service as a gardener. ("In The Hands Of The Prophets")

I've been doing this for 30 years. I am not an overnight discovery. -
—Rene Auberjonois

VEDEK WINN

(Louise Fletcher) A high-ranking Bajoran religious official, also a cleric in the Bajoran orthodox order. She is a tough woman in her 60's and makes it known that she is in line to be Kai. She interrupts Keiko's class and accuses her of teaching blasphemous material and decides to put a stop to it. She often resorts to thinly-veiled threats. Her followers are responsible for blowing up the school, and her co-conspirator, Neela, O'Brien's assistant, tried to assassinate Vedek Bareil under Vedek Winn's instructions. ("In The Hands Of The Prophets")

VELOS SEVEN INTERNMENT CAMP

Cardassian prison camp for Bajoran terrorists and prisoners. Dekon Elig was incarcerated there and killed during an escape attempt. He was pronounced dead by Dr.

Surmak Ren who was also imprisoned there. ("Babel")

VENDOR

(Michael Eugene Fairman)

Merchant on the Promenade that sells Jumja sticks, but refuses to sell one to O'Brien. ("In The Hands Of The Prophets")

VERTRONS

Unique self-sustaining particles that were used by the Prophet entities in constructing the wormhole. ("In The Hands Of The Prophets")

VERATH SYSTEM

Star system in the Gamma Quadrant whose civilization reached its height 30 thousand years ago. It was made up of two dozen systems connected by a highly developed trade and communications system. Vash brought back a stone statue from there which represents Drolock, the Prime

Asemety of the 19th Dynasty. ("Q-Less")

VOLCHOK PRIME

Planet where Ferengi Hoex bought out rival Ferengi Turot's interest in the cargo port. ("The Nagus")

W

WADI

A newly discovered race from the Gamma Quadrant who visit DS9. The Wadi have exotic facial markings and love to play games. They were discovered three weeks previously by a Vulcan vessel. ("Move Along Home")

WANONI TRACE-HOUND

Type of canine that aggressively pursues its prey. Odo compares Lwaxana Troi to one. ("The Forsaken")

WARP CORE

Damage to containment field of the warp core caused destruction of the U.S.S. Saratoga in the Borg attack. ("Emissary")

WEAPON'S LOCKER

Storage area on DS9 for weapons. It is located in the Habitat Ring, Level 5, Section 3. It is restricted to Security Level seven and above. ("Captive Pursuit")

WILLIAMS, TED

Twentieth-century baseball great mentioned by Quark as one of the players Jake plays with in the holosuite. ("If Wishes Were Horses")

WOBAN

(Jordan Lund) Leader of the Bajoran clan, the Navot. ("The Storyteller")

WOLF 359

Location of battle between the Borg ship and forty Federation ships, including the

Melbourne, the Gage, the Kyushu, Tolstoi, ("Emissary") (novelization) and the Saratoga, Ben Sisko's ship. All forty Federation ships were destroyed in one of the greatest massacres in Starfleet's history. ("Emissary")

WOO, PROFESSOR

Scientist at the Daystrom Institute who once suspended Vash's membership from the Institute's archaeological council. ("Q-Less")

WORMHOLE

Stable space phenomenon, which can transport a ship from the Bajor star system in the Alpha Quadrant (("Captive Pursuit")) to the Gamma Quadrant. Sensors cease functioning and all contact with the space-station is lost, along with all navigational functions. The closest star system on the Gamma Quadrant end is Idran, seventy thousand light-years from Bajor. This particular Wormhole is different, in that it is stable and lacks all the usual residence waves. In Sisko's initial encounter, he and Dax landed some place inside the Wormhole and were greeted by a Tear of the Prophet orb which probed them with a low-level ionic pattern, and sent Sisko into more flashback sequences to communicate with the Wormhole inhabitants. Entrance into and departure from is accompanied by a neutrino disturbance. ("Emissary")

DS9 would be torn to bits if it tried to enter the Wormhole. ("Q-Less")

The Wormhole can only be seen when a ship either enters or exits it. ("Battle Lines")

The Toh'Kaht emerged from the Wormhole over a month early, bringing back a disease that made everyone confrontational. ("Dramatis Personae")

A strange probe entered the Alpha Quadrant from there. It contains the 'Pup' computer lifeform. ("The Forsaken")

According to Keiko in her classroom, the Wormhole was formed by unique particles called vertrons that are apparently self-sustaining. Ships must be using impulse power to move through the Wormhole. ("In The Hands Of The Prophets")

WORMHOLE INHABITANTS

Intelligent beings who control and possibly constructed the Wormhole. Regarded by the Bajorans as Prophets, the beings have no concept of 'time,' something Sisko tries to explain to them. Originally they wished to destroy him, but later, after he proves himself, they allow passage to all through the Wormhole. ("Emissary")

WRAPPAGES

Serving of Yamok sauce. ("Progress")

Y

YADOZI DESERT

Odo mentions the desert in an example. It is apparently next to impossible to find a drink of water there. ("A Man Alone")

YAMOK SAUCE

Cardassian condiment that is worthless to anyone other than Cardassians. A waiter in Quark's mistakenly ordered five-thousand wrappages of original, not replicated Yamok sauce. ("Progress")

One of its uses is on Sem'hal Stew. ("Duet")

YANGTZEE, KIANG

Federation Runabout used by Major Kira and

crew to attempt to rescue Sisko from the wormhole. ("Emissary") Also used by Tahna Los in his terrorist attempt to destroy the wormhole. ("Past Prologue") For Kai Opaka's trip through the wormhole, this Runabout was used to carry the Kai, Kira, Sisko, and Bashir to a Gamma Quadrant moon. It crash landed there and was destroyed. ("Battle Lines")

YARETH

Daughter of the Rahkari criminal Croden and the only survivor of his family. She was allowed to escape with her father and travel to Vulcan. ("Vortex")

YUGADA

A Wadi Word. ("Move Along Home")

Z

ZARRO

Computer readout shows this person had a scheduled meeting with Ibudan concerning project analysis. ("A Man Alone")

ZAYRA

Bajoran who runs the Transit Aid Center on DS9. ("A Man Alone")

ZEK

(Wallace Shawn) Very old leader of the Ferengi, he loves spending time in the holo-suites. He comes to DS9 to host a Ferengi economic summit, and to step down from his position as Nagus, because he says, "I'm just not as greedy as I used to be." A surprise to everyone, especially his son Krax, Quark is named his successor. He soon fakes death, through a sleeping

trance, to test his son. He claims he hasn't had a vacation in eighty-five years. ("The Nagus")

ZLANGCO

(Paul Collins) Leader of the Nol-Ennis, a people at war on a penal colony in the Gamma Quadrant. ("Battle Lines")

This glossary just covers season one of DEEP SPACE NINE, but if you want to read up on the entire STAR TREK universe then check out Pioneer Book's STAR TREK ENCY-CLOPEDIA by Wendy Rathbone, new for 1994!

THE HISTORY OF TREK

James Van Hise

The complete story of Star Trek from Original conception to its effects on millions of Lives across the world. This book celebrates the 25th anniversary of the first "Star Trek" television episode and traces the history of the show that has become an enduring legend—even the non-Trekkies can quote specific lines and characters from the original television series. The History of Trek chronicles "Star Trek" from its start in 1966 to its cancellation in 1969; discusses the lean years when "Star Trek" wasn't shown on television but legions of die hard fans kept interest in it still alive; covers the sequence of five successful movies (and includes the upcoming sixth one); and reviews "The Next Generation" television series, now entering its sixth season. Complete with Photographs, The History of Trek reveals the origins of the first series in interviews with the original cast and creative staff. It also takes readers behind the scenes of all six Star Trek movies, offers a wealth of Star Trek Trivia, and speculates on what the future may hold.

$14.95.....160 Pages
ISBN # 1-55698-309-3

THE MAN BETWEEN THE EARS:
STAR TREKS LEONARD NIMOY

James Van Hise

Based on his numerous interviews with Leonard Nimoy, Van Hise tells the story of the man as well as the entertainer.

This book chronicles the many talents of Leonard Nimoy from the beginning of his career in Boston to his latest starring work in the movie, Never Forget. His 25-year association with Star Trek is the centerpiece, but his work outside the Starship Enterprise is also covered, from such early efforts as Zombies of the Stratosphere to his latest directorial and acting work, and his stage debut in Vermont.

$14.95.....160 Pages
ISBN # 1-55698-304-2

COUCH POTATO INC. 5715 N. Balsam Rd Las Vegas, NV 89130 (702)658-2090

Use Your Credit Card 24 HRS — Order toll Free From: **(800)444-2524** Ext 67

TREK: THE MAKING OF THE MOVIES

James Van Hise

TREK: THE MAKING OF THE MOVIES tells the complete story both on-screen and behind the scenes of the biggest STAR TREK adventures of all. Plus the story of the STAR TREK II that never happened and the aborted STAR TREK VI: STARFLEET ACADEMY.

$14.95.....160 Pages
ISBN # 1-55698-313-1

TREK: THE LOST YEARS

Edward Gross

The tumultouos, behind-the-scenes saga of this modern day myth between the cancellation of the original series in 1969 and the announcement of the first movie ten years later. In addition, the text explores the scripts and treatments written throughout the 1970's, including every proposed theatrical feature and an episode guide for STAR TREK II, with comments from the writers whose efforts would ultimately never reach the screen.

This volume came together after years of research, wherein the author interviewed a wide variety of people involved with every aborted attempt at revival, from story editors to production designers to David Gautreaux, the actor signed to replace Leonard Nimoy; and had access to exclusive resource material, including memos and correspondences, as well as teleplays and script outlines.

$12.95.....132 Pages
ISBN # 1-55698-220-8

COUCH POTATO INC.   5715 N. Balsam Rd   Las Vegas, NV 89130   (702)658-2090

Use Your Credit Card 24 HRS — Order toll Free From: **(800)444-2524** Ext 67

BORING, BUT NECESSARY ORDERING INFORMATION

Payment:

Use our new 800 # and pay with your credit card or send check or money order directly to our address. All payments must be made in U.S. funds and please do not send cash.

Shipping:

We offer several methods of shipment. Sometimes a book can be delayed if we are temporarily out of stock. You should note whether you prefer us to ship the book as soon as available, send you a merchandise credit good for other goodies, or send your money back immediately.

Normal Post Office: $3.75 for the first book and $1.50 for each additional book. These orders are filled as quickly as possible. Shipments normally take 5 to 10 days, but allow up to 12 weeks for delivery.

Special UPS 2 Day Blue Label Service or Priority Mail: Special service is available for desperate Couch Potatoes. These books are shipped within 24 hours of when we receive the order and normally take 2 to 3 three days to get to you. The cost is $10.00 for the first book and $4.00 each additional book .

Overnight Rush Service: $20.00 for the first book and $10.00 each additional book.

U.s. Priority Mail: $6.00 for the first book and $3.00.each additional book.

Canada And Mexico: $5.00 for the first book and $3.00 each additional book.

Foreign: $6.00 for the first book and $3.00 each additional book.

Please list alternatives when available and please state if you would like a refund or for us to backorder an item if it is not in stock.

ORDER FORM

_____ Trek Crew Book $9.95
_____ Best Of Enterprise Incidents $9.95
_____ Trek Fans Handbook $9.95
_____ Trek: The Next Generation $14.95
_____ The Man Who Created Star Trek: $12.95
_____ 25th Anniversary Trek Tribute $14.95
_____ History Of Trek $14.95
_____ The Man Between The Ears $14.95
_____ Trek: The Making Of The Movies $14.95
_____ Trek: The Lost Years $12.95
_____ Trek: The Unauthorized Next Generation $14.95
_____ New Trek Encyclopedia $19.95
_____ Making A Quantum Leap $14.95
_____ The Unofficial Tale Of Beauty And The Beast $14.95
_____ Complete Lost In Space $19.95
_____ ..doctor Who Encyclopedia: Baker $19.95
_____ Lost In Space Tribute Book $14.95
_____ Lost In Space With Irwin Allen $14.95
_____ Doctor Who: Baker Years $19.95
_____ Doctor Who: Pertwee Years $19.95
_____ Batmania Ii $14.95
_____ The Green Hornet $14.95 _____ Special Edition $16.95

_____ Number Six: The Prisoner Book $14.95
_____ Gerry Anderson: Supermarionation $17.95
_____ Addams Family Revealed $14.95
_____ Bloodsucker: Vampires At The Movies $14.95
_____ Dark Shadows Tribute $14.95
_____ Monsterland Fear Book $14.95
_____ The Films Of Elvis $14.95
_____ The Woody Allen Encyclopedia $14.95
_____ Paul Mccartney: 20 Years On His Own $9.95
_____ Yesterday: My Life With The Beatles $14.95
_____ Fab Films Of The Beatles $14.95
_____ 40 Years At Night: The Tonight Show $14.95
_____ Exposing Northern Exposure $14.95
_____ The La Lawbook $14.95
_____ Cheers: Where Everybody Knows Your Name $14.95
_____ SNL! The World Of Saturday Night Live $14.95
_____ The Rockford Phile $14.95
_____ Encyclopedia Of Cartoon Superstars $14.95
_____ How To Create Animation $14.95
_____ How To Draw Art For Comic Books $14.95
_____ King And Barker:an Illustrated Guide $14.95
_____ King And Barker: An Illustrated Guide II $14.95

100% Satisfaction Guaranteed.

We value your support. You will receive a full refund as long as the copy of the book you are not happy with is received back by us in reasonable condition. No questions asked, except we would like to know how we failed you. Refunds and credits are given as soon as we receive back the item you do not want.

NAME:_____

STREET:_____

CITY:_____

STATE:_____

ZIP:_____

TOTAL:_____ SHIPPING_____

SEND TO: Couch Potato, Inc. 5715 N. Balsam Rd., Las Vegas, NV 89130